Of Love and Peace

Light Passers Chronicles books:

Quest of the Chosen—The Journey Begins (Book 1): This foundational first book, like *The Hobbit*, introduces the series, but also serves as a standalone mystical adventure, packed with action, danger, and self-discovery.

OtherLight—The Quest Continues (Book 2): Set in Jerusalem, this story brings the heroes of *Quest of the Chosen* into a real-life setting, incorporating history and philosophy while maintaining the cornerstone elements of a mystery thriller.

Of Love and Peace

A Light Passers Novel

BOOK 2.5

Bruce Campelia

ISBN: 979-8-9866656-4-1

PRINTED IN THE UNITED STATES OF AMERICA

This book is dedicated to the frontline nurses and doctors, first responders, medics, support staff, and all other guardians of life, love, and peace throughout the many thousand years of human civilization. Blessings to all for sacrificing so much of your time, and often your lives in service to others, and for your contribution in helping heal the unrelenting self-inflicted wounds resulting from humankind's shared struggle to survive. You have my total admiration, honor, and respect.

"When the power of love overcomes the love of power, the world will know peace."

– Jimi Hendrix

Preface

WHILE WRITING *Of Love & Peace,* I was often reminded of the devastating toll on innocent lives taken by fear-incited war, aggression, ignorance, and the self-serving of others.

In this book, the use of the term *The Levant* focuses on Israel and Palestine—but the name traditionally also includes Syria, Lebanon, Jordan, and Cyprus, and is one of the earliest cradles of the human experience of building societies to work together to better humankind. It is a region that has seen many wars, but also long periods of shared *community* as a land of immigrants. It can be credited as an early example of how people of different religions and spiritual beliefs who migrated there from Europe, Africa, and Eastern lands over tens of thousands of years have worked together in love and peace…and could again.

Since the end of WWII, and especially today, the Levant has been thrown into political and spiritual turmoil, resulting in incomprehensible pain and suffering. The primary two groups seeking to reestablish a more stable, permanent homeland have been the Israelis and Palestinians. Recent extreme religious and political beliefs and outside interference have soured the hope for the Levant to be as it was: a land of mutual respect and honor, and a beacon for the world—an example for all to follow, once more.

Recent developments have led to the extremely brutal and unnecessary deaths of Israeli and Palestinian men, women, and children. Tens of thousands of innocents…most who never wanted any war but just to be treated fairly and live their lives as any family, parent, or child would strive for—in *happiness, love, and peace.* The greed, selfishness, and clear lack of concern by leaders on both sides shows contempt for the foundations on which their own religions were built. This betrays the gifts given to them by their ancestors, and the clear instructions that they be passed on to future generations.

Those who are forced to witness this the most are the responders to whom I refer in the dedication and all those who support them in their mission. They begin the healing by saving those who lie under and in the rubble in the bombed-out streets, buildings, and even hospitals, and continue it by caring for those still suffering from hurt or illness.

I, personally, have been honored by the presence of such heroes in my very family. My father, Vincent Campelia, was an oral surgeon and dentist in WWII. He was a Major in the US Army as staff to General George S. Patton. He operated in a MASH unit during the battles of North Africa, and then under General Mark Clarke in Italy where he lived and performed facial and other surgeries underground for four months during the Battle of Anzio, one of the most brutal battles of the war.

He suffered PTSD (unidentified at the time) for many years after he returned home to New England. I once found him late at night curled up under his bed—screaming and covering his head with his arms. During his dental practice outside of Boston, he never made a poor person pay for the help he gave them. One man drove all the way from New York to see him. I was twenty at the time, painting one of the rooms in his office area when the man walked in, and I overheard him speaking with my dad's assistant. He told her how grateful he was and that there was no man like my father. When he stepped out of the office, I sensed my eyes welling up.

So, my father was one of these heroes I speak of—like the surgeons, doctors, first responders, staff, and others who assist Palestinian patients in bombed-out hospitals in Gaza or try to save innocent Israelis caught in the murderous assault on kibbutzim like Re'im in southern Israel.

My mother, Clarice Campelia, was a nurse at the Hartford Hospital in Connecticut before the war, where she met my dad who was an intern at the time. She continued as an RN during the war and as a member of the US Naval Reserve. She gave up her nursing to raise a family but returned to service when we grew up, not as a nurse this time but as a librarian to help children learn…she loved the "little ones" she would say.

The mother of my children, Linda Campelia, is a semi-retired Adult Nurse Practitioner who worked for Massachusetts General Hospital (MGH) in Boston on an open ward for poor patients, as well as in the Cardiac Care Unit (CCU) and Intensive Care Unit (ICU). She was a nurse her entire career, even when we were raising three girls. She, too, gave a lifetime to service and has a soft spot for kids.

My daughter, Alexis Lampros, is a Family Nurse Practitioner working part-time as she and her husband raise three young children of their own. She, too, was a nurse at MGH, serving on the pediatric floor and helping children recover from traumatic surgeries, psychiatric and neurological illnesses, cancer, gunshot wounds, and burns. Too many of these kids never recovered at all—so young…so much ahead they were never to see. Knowing her, I think she probably cried every time. She received a commendation in the Boston Globe. And she is also one of these heroes.

All those in the Levant today, and humans throughout the world, who serve others in this way, or any way, where they put the other above themselves are simply saints. And we should all aspire to be like them. To put others first…to walk in the Light—the only path out of our collective darkness.

Author Note

Of Love & Peace is a fast-paced short follow-on novel to *OtherLight.* Along with *Quest of the Chosen,* it establishes an exciting three-book mini-series based on the long history and today's troubled times in Israel and Palestine—referred to as The Levant. It is also a companion book to the Light Passers Chronicles five-book main series.

The close mix of fact and fiction, using both real and fictional names and settings, is intended to deliver the credibility, pace, and urgency of reality while maintaining the intricate balance of a modern-day mystery/thriller.

This is my third book and was written to build off of *OtherLight* because I felt the events that have unfolded in Israel and Palestine over recent years necessitated this. I wanted to elevate the issues while also proposing a vision of perhaps the only real way true and permanent change can quell the volatile powder keg that is the Middle East—especially in Palestine and Israel. And serve as a paradigm for healing the world.

Book four (which will be book three of the main five-book series) is underway and is planned for release in the spring of 2025.

ISRAEL
יִשְׂרָאֵל
إسرائيل
LEBANON
Golan Heights
SYRIA
Sea of Galilee
Galilee
Coastal Plain
Tel Aviv
Jordan
WEST BANK (PALESTINE)
Jerusalem
Bethlehem
Jordan Rift Valley
MEDITERRANEAN SEA
ISRAEL
Dead Sea
GAZA STRIP (PALESTINE)
A.I.A
Beersheba
Negev Desert
JORDAN
EGYPT
ISRAEL

GAZA STRIP
רצועת עזה
قطاع غزة

Beit Lahia
Erez
Jabalia
Beit Hanoun
Gaza
MEDITERRANEAN SEA
Deir al-Balah
ISRAEL
LEBANON
SYRIA
MEDITERRANEAN SEA
Re'im
West Bank
Khan Yunis
Abasan al-Kabera
ISRAEL
Rafah
JORDAN
Arafat Int'l Airport
EGYPT
EGYPT

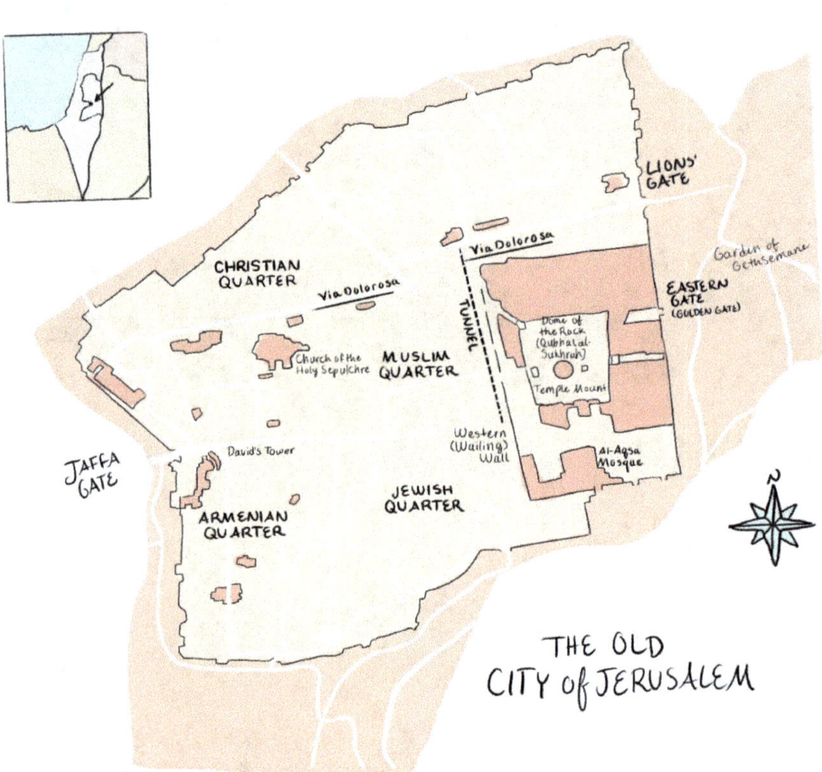
LIONS' GATE
Via Dolorosa
Garden of Gethsemane
CHRISTIAN QUARTER
Via Dolorosa
EASTERN GATE (GOLDEN GATE)
TUNNEL
Dome of the Rock (Qubbat al-Sukhrah)
Church of the Holy Sepulchre
MUSLIM QUARTER
Temple Mount
Western (Wailing) Wall
David's Tower
Al-Aqsa Mosque
JAFFA GATE
JEWISH QUARTER
ARMENIAN QUARTER
N
THE OLD CITY of JERUSALEM

Characters, Places & More

Characters*:

Liyah: Teen girl from Gaza, Palestine
Esty: Israeli teen girl and tourist guide
Ahmad: Palestinian teen boy
Nura: Young mysterious woman loved by Palestinians
Khalib: Liyah's younger brother
Hanna: Esty's longtime Jewish friend
Malik: Ex-Hamas leader
Daniel (Dan) Campbell: American student studying archaeology in Jerusalem
Ali: Khalib's friend
Jawad: Khalib's friend
David Al-Rahim: Liyah's father and owner of the Filastin Dawn paper
Rania Al-Rahim: Liyah's mother
Dr. Adam Blum: Esty's father and consultant to the Prime Minister of Israel
Hawk: Keeper of the gate to the main tunnel in northern Gaza

Original Founding Light Passer Team:
Morningstar: Lakota Sioux teen
Zack: Black teen from Detroit
Liyah: Teen girl from Palestine
Kai Li: Asian teen from Hong Kong
Ooray: Mystical Being

*Note: All names of individuals are fictional

Places, groups, and other information

Kibbutz: Name for communal living groups, towns, in Israel
Kibbutzim: Plural of kibbutz
Hijab: Head covering worn by Muslim women
IDF: Israeli Defense Forces
Prime Minister: Head of the Israeli government
Hamas: Palestinian extreme Islamist political and military group in the Gaza Strip
Dolomites: Mountain range in the Alps of northeastern Italy
Jerusalem: One of the oldest cities in the world, and a spiritual center for Judaism, Christianity, and Islam
Old City: Oldest part of Jerusalem located on the Temple Mount
Church of the Holy Sepulcher: Church in the Christian Quarter of the Old City
Dome of the Rock: Islamic shrine located on the Temple Mount
Al-Aqsa Mosque: Mosque compound located in the Old City
Western Wall (sometimes referred to as the Wailing Wall): Ancient wall in the Old City
Gaza Strip: Small, densely populated Palestinian territory on Israel's southern border.
The Negev: Desert in southern Israel
West Bank: Palestinian territory bordering Israel to the East
Bible: Holy text of Christianity
Quran: Holy text of Islam
Talmud: Holy Text of Judaism
Zah-re: ('zah-ray') - Book of Truths: Fictional summary writings representing universal truths

ONE

THE EARLY FALL sun stole through the gap between the window curtains and slowly crept along the side of Liyah's face. Eyes still closed, her body stirred. A moment later, her eyelids blinked open, and the ceiling came into focus. A new day had begun.

Sliding out of bed, she checked the clock on her bureau: 8:42 a.m. Early for her for a Sunday, but actually a welcome end to the dream she was having about being lost in a forest and unable to find her friends. She picked up the clothes she had placed the night before on the small chest at the foot of her bed: jeans, black cotton shift, clean underwear, low white socks, and slip-on white trainers.

Making her way to the bathroom, she threw cold water on her face, donned her outfit, brushed her hair, then headed down the stairs. Soft classical music from the den filled her ears and the aroma of hummus, fresh apricots, and za'atar—a spice with thyme, drifted down the hall from the dining room.

Liyah entered the kitchen. Her mother stood at the sink, water running, with a peeler in one hand and a piece of fruit in the other.

"Morning Mama!"

"Ya, Allah!" her mom cried out, jerking her head around, then pointing the peeler at her. "Don't sneak up on me like that, Liyah."

"Sorry. I thought you heard me come in." She peered into the dining room. "Where's Khalib?"

"Where have you been? He's fourteen. We're lucky to see him before eleven…It's even early for you isn't it?"

"Sort of, I guess."

"Well, grab a plate and some juice. There's bread, some goat cheese, fruit, and dip on the table. I'll fix a bowl of oatmeal for you."

Liyah poured a glass of orange juice and headed into the dining room. "No need for the oatmeal, Mama. Not really that hungry yet."

"You should eat more," her mother commented quietly as Liyah took her seat at the table.

"I heard that," Liyah called back.

"Well, I worry about you dear."

"I'm not twelve, you know."

"Yes, well sometimes I think so. You seem to be out of sorts lately."

"Oh, Mama," Liyah let out a loud sigh.

"And I heard that."

"Okay, Okay. It's too early for this."

"Good morning, Habibti," Liyah's dad said as he wandered into the dining room.

Liyah looked up and nodded. "Hi, Baba. I thought maybe you were into your music."

A warm smile broadened across his face. "I was. But I always have time for my favorite daughter."

Liyah laughed. "Only daughter."

He returned the laugh. "Yes, well…mind if I join you?" He took the chair across from her.

"So, what's on your mind, Baba? You only do this if you have something important to say." She squinted her eyes. "Did I do something wrong?"

"No, no. So untrusting, aren't we?"

Liyah smiled. "You forget, Baba. I know you."

"Ah, well…on that note. Yes, there is something. But it's not you."

Liyah noticed her mom had left the kitchen and was standing in the archway between the two rooms. She glanced over at her, back to her dad, then back again to her mom. "Must be *really* serious," she said, half joking. When neither one said anything right away, Liyah's eyes narrowed, and her face took on a somber look.

"David?" her mom prodded.

He was tapping his fingers on the table. He stopped and studied his daughter briefly.

"It has to do with the incident we reported in yesterday's late edition of *The Filastin Dawn*."

"You mean the attack on the civilians near the border in Israel?"

"Yes. Exactly."

"I'm already aware of that, Baba. There weren't many details I thought. Something new?"

He glanced at his wife, briefly holding eye contact, then brought his attention back to Liyah. "Unfortunately, yes."

"Well? Why are you dragging this out? Jeez, Baba!"

"It was more than an isolated incident, sweetie. It was planned by Hamas and several other groups." He breathed deeply. "In addition to the thousands of missiles we knew about that were fired at the typical targets throughout Israel, they launched a coordinated assault involving the breaching of the border along Gaza by armed militants."

Liyah was wide-eyed. "Allah!" she exclaimed in a hush of her breath.

"Yes," her mother replied. "Indeed."

"It gets worse," her father added. He locked onto his daughter's eyes. A grave sadness infiltrated his countenance. "It included a massacre at the music festival near Re'im and at several kibbutzim, as well as other places along the border. There was killing, raping, and kidnapping of girls, women, boys, and men…even children and babies weren't spared. There are early estimates that perhaps over a thousand people were killed and several hundred taken as hostages."

Liyah stared across the table at him in silence.

He continued. "I was up very early this morning and went in to work. We have twenty-four-hour coverage of course, and I need to rally the team. I just came home for a late breakfast and will be headed back in shortly. I wanted you to hear this from *me* before I get tied up with the staff at work, or you hear it from other media coverage that are now swarming all over the place to hear the latest developments. I'll be spending a lot of time at the Dawn."

Liyah caught the seriousness of his tone. She studied him. His eyes alone already betrayed the weight of the situation on him. He appeared tired, even after only one early morning of dealing with getting out an early edition. It was his responsibility to report the news fairly to not only those who lived in Gaza but to the world. He had the ears of both sides of the continuing and seemingly unresolvable conflict in the region. And his employees at the

Dawn, his "baby," the paper he started so many years ago, would rely on his leadership…again. *Would the paper once more be a target of radicals who only wanted to escalate the conflict?* Her mind flashed back for an instant to the time when she was just a child and radicals threw a bomb into their home, burying her in debris.

But this situation felt different than times past to Liyah. She knew this wasn't just another barrage of missiles blindly hurled at Israel by Hamas, then shot down by the Iron Dome defense system with little destruction. It was bigger. Much bigger!

It had been only a handful of months since she and her friends stood on the top of the Wailing Wall in East Jerusalem and helped save everyone from a new kind of attack, a plot by Hamas and other radical players in the region. But this was not the same; yes Hamas, and yes many of the other players. But more horrific, as her dad just had described it: the insane brutality of it, the kidnapping, the targeting of the helpless.

Liyah's mind whirled, as she poked the pieces of fruit on her plate with her fork. *What did it all mean? What would happen next? What about the mission she was on with her new friends—Morningstar and Zack from America, and Kai Li from Hong Kong? And then there was Esty to consider. Her father was an advisor to the Prime Minister of Israel. The families had become bound together after that last episode. Weren't they all the new warriors of peace? The hope for Palestine and Israel? An example for the world?*

Her eyes remained locked on her dad's. Her mind slowed. *Had it all been just a dream…a shattered one now at that?*

She sighed, then reached for her father's hand, taking it in hers. "What's gonna happen now, Baba?

"Only Allah knows, sweetie. But I *will* say it doesn't look good. There's no doubt Israel will retaliate. But in what way?" He looked over at his wife, then back to his daughter. "I cannot even guess at what lies ahead. No one here in Gaza can. But we will know soon…very soon."

"What about Esty's dad? Liyah questioned. "Can't he help? Or can't he at least tell us what is likely?"

"I'm going to call Adam from the office when I get back to the Dawn. He's been put in an awkward position now. So, I don't expect much. But I haven't spoken with him for a while, and it will be good to get in touch…keep the channels open so to speak at this critical time."

Liyah's mom stood up, pushing her chair back. "Best thing to do is keep busy until the next shoe drops." She turned and headed back into the kitchen, still talking. "No sense in worrying about it since there's nothing we can do. And besides, Liyah, I need you to pick up a few things for us for the week at the market."

Two

THERE WAS A loud rap on the office door.

"Come in," David Al-Rahim called out as he finished shuffling some papers on his desk.

The door swung open.

"Ahmad! Thanks for responding so quickly. We have a lot to do. I appreciate you coming in on a Sunday."

Ahmad approached his desk. "No Problem, sir. Everyone is very nervous. What can I do to help?"

Liyah's father looked up at the strong young man who had been an apprentice journalist for such a short time, and who was one of the key players in saving Jerusalem during the surprise attacks on the Old City during last spring's holy celebrations of Ramadan, Christmas, and Passover.

"I understand you've heard the news about the attacks?"

"Yes."

"It's going to get very intense around here. We are going to need all hands on deck, overtime, and on weekends for a bit."

"I'm game, sir."

"Okay, great. First off, I was wondering if you've been staying in touch with some of the people you met with before, who you were able to get information from for the article you wrote the day after the events in the Old City. Like the Iranian who did the falcon training, or was he a Saudi? Or that leader from Hamas…Hassan I think was his name."

"The falconer's name was Yusuf. He left just before the assault on the Old City. I haven't heard anything since then. We believe he may have returned to his home city of Tehran. And Hassan has dropped out of site, either for his own safety after his part in the spring attacks failed…or maybe he was *put out of commission* by Hamas, themselves."

"Hmm. Well, see what you can find out about where the hostages may have been taken, any Hamas plans whatsoever. But don't get yourself killed. Right?"

"Right, sir."

Liyah's dad stood up and walked Ahmad to the door. "I appreciate anything you can find out. It's critical to everyone that we help try to lower the temperature of this, but expose the truth at the same time, if you know what I mean."

"I do, sir."

"Oh, and one other thing, Ahmad," his boss said as he started to close the door behind Ahmad, "Have you heard much from Esty on this? I understand she knows a few people as well."

"Why would she say anything to me, sir?"

"Come on, Ahmad," his boss chuckled. "Liyah told me you two were an item. I didn't notice at the time when we all had dinner together at my home to celebrate everyone's contribution to saving the Old City. But then I tend to be oblivious about these things."

Ahmad's face flushed. "Oh, well…I don't know, sir. She's a wonderful girl but…uh…you might have better luck with her dad."

"Yes, yes, Ahmad. Well, say hello to Esty when you see her anyway."

Liyah's dad laughed again as he closed the door and made his way back to his desk. He sat down in his chair, picked up the phone, and called Esty's father's home number.

"Hello."

"Hello, Adam. It's David."

"Ah. So nice to hear from you. I was actually thinking of giving you a buzz. It's been a while."

"Yes. My apologies. I think I owed you a call…been a bit busy the last few weeks."

"Not to worry, David. I should have called myself. What can I do for you?"

Liyah's dad reclined the swivel leather chair and put his feet up on his desk. "Well, I didn't want to bother you on a Sunday, but the recent developments with Hamas have certainly caught everyone's attention, and I felt maybe you'd be getting busier than ever. That is, given your position as advisor to the Prime Minister and having the ear of members of the Cabinet."

"It's more than awful, isn't it, David? Is there something specific I can help you with?"

"Actually, I'm just generally concerned about what's happening, especially since it was apparent our two sides were making a lot of progress after the trouble last spring. I still have a hard time believing some of the things that happened then. But they gave us hope…those youngsters of ours. Didn't they?"

"No doubt about it, David. And you're right…it was like a *shift* had begun. Exciting, actually."

"I'm not prodding for a story, Adam. I would never do that to you. Besides, that's the job of our reporters."

Adam chuckled. "Well speaking of reporters, Ahmad's been chatting it up with Esty almost every day since the celebration dinner at your place, after they and your own daughter pretty much saved the city."

"Ahmad and Esty? Really?"

"Oh, c'mon David. Don't tell me you're blind. They couldn't help glancing at each other the whole evening."

"I had no…"

His friend almost choked on his laughter. "It's all good, David. I look at it as kind of a Romeo and Juliet thing. They're entranced with each other but are caught up by opposing sides. You know, like feuding families."

"Liyah's dad laughed lightly into the handset in acknowledgment. "I see. The Capulets and the Montagues. Perhaps you're right. Ahmad has been acting a bit goofy lately and stuffs his cell phone in his pocket at times when I enter the room."

"Exactly, David. But Esty isn't as subtle. I hear her chatting his name with her friends and see his name scribbled all over her notepads. And she thinks I'm *oblivious*. Kids!"

Liyah's dad grinned. "I get it, Adam," he replied, before becoming more serious. "I guess what I'm looking for is anything I should know for my family's sake…like if we're safe here in northern Gaza. Specifically at our house in Beit Lahia."

"From the sound of it, you must be somewhere else now. I'm assuming maybe the Filastin Dawn?"

"Yeah. You can imagine."

"I can indeed. You must be a busy guy given the urgent state of affairs. I'm likely to be called into the emergency meeting of the Cabinet today, myself."

"What are you hearing? I'm not asking you to divulge anything secret, or even sensitive. Just your thoughts on how this all might evolve."

"Don't worry, David. I wouldn't say anything I wasn't allowed to say anyway. And I certainly trust you, even if I give a slip of the tongue. At the moment I actually don't know much more than anyone else. I'm getting my news from people like you." He let out a low laugh. "The attacks occurred yesterday morning and not many people seemed to know much about them until later in the afternoon…some sort of gaff by the defense forces it seems to me. But the IDF hasn't said anything, formally, and I haven't been called in yet. I do know, however, that they are meeting now with the Prime Minister, and that there will be a briefing to the full Cabinet shortly."

"What about the hostages? Any word on them?"

"No names yet. You've probably heard the initial estimates, and some of the details of just how awful the whole thing must have been at the time…and now continues with the hostages. If the reports are true, no one is going to excuse the inhumanity of this, even those here in Israel who believe we are actively stealing lands from Palestinians in the West Bank."

"I'm deeply saddened by the whole thing, Adam. Deeply. I never expected Hamas to go to this level of brutality. And I thought we were structuring a new way forward between Israelis and Palestinians."

"Well, this is going to put more than one fly in the ointment, for sure," replied Esty's father. "And then we still don't know what the Israeli government's response will be, or when this all might end. It's a tragedy already, and I fear it is only going to get worse…at least into the near future."

"If you hear anything you can tell me the line is always open, Adam. And let's plan a time for the two families to get together again. It's been too long."

"Sure thing, David. We'll plan something soon. Say hello to your lovely wife Rania for me."

"Yes, I will. Be well, my friend."

"Mr. Rahim," said the receptionist, as Liyah's dad entered the foyer after being out for lunch. "There's a message for you from Dr. Blum."

"Thanks. I'll get it right away."

He grabbed the receiver while still standing and pushed the lighted message button.

Hello again David. It's Adam. Thought I would catch you. An hour after we spoke, I received a message from the Prime Minister. We have declared war on Hamas. Sorry to bring such bad news to your doorstep. I'm headed to Tel Aviv now. I'll be in touch with any important updates. Stay safe and don't be afraid to call me anytime.

Three

LIYAH WAS PLACING the last of the supplies away in the cabinets after returning from the market. Her mother appeared in the kitchen. She turned to face her, holding a cereal box in one hand.

"Hi, Mama."

"Habibti, is something the matter? You haven't been yourself today. Is it the news about the situation across the border?"

"Mostly, I guess. It's awful, for sure. But it's also different from the random attacks and retaliations by both Hamas and Israel over recent years. It's not only gruesome, it's personal."

"What do you mean, dear?"

Liyah placed the box in the cupboard and closed it. Then turned back again.

"I mean killing people hand to hand is the most personal kind of killing, don't you think? You can drop a bomb from and airplane or hurl a missile into a neighborhood, but there's a distance that separates you from your intended victims…It gives you a kind of *excuse*, doesn't it?"

"I suppose so, if you put it that way," her mother replied blankly, appearing to be caught off guard by the question. "But you still know people will die."

"Yes, Mama, but you don't know who because you don't see their faces. You don't drive the knife in or watch their face the moment before you shoot them in the head." She watched as her mother grimaced.

"Goodness, Liyah! That's awful."

"Yes, well it's worse for the child, the mother, the boy, the father. They end up dead."

"Now I see why you're walking around with your face on the floor. You need to stop thinking those terrible thoughts."

"The problem is I can't seem to. And if I can't, what do you think the Israelis are going to think? It's not going to be sadness…more like massive hatred for all of us in Gaza. For any Palestinian."

"But it's not us, Liyah." Her mother took hold of her arm. "It's Hamas."

"We know that. Baba knows that. And many Palestinians know that. Yet many others still side with Hamas as well. Too many, I fear."

"But you and Esty have done well in showing the way since the trouble in Jerusalem. People admire both of you. They see you as symbols of hope…perhaps a new day coming for all of us."

Liyah hugged her. "Thanks, Mama. I really appreciate it. But even on that she and I have been falling down. We haven't seen each other for a month. It's like we're stalled and running out of gas. And I don't know how to get untracked, especially now with this new crap happening."

"Liyah!"

"Sorry. But it's just, well, *everything*, I guess. Even the weather knows."

Her mother frowned. "The weather?"

"Yeah, I mean the sun came out this morning I thought it would be a great day. But then there was the news. And when I was at the market the sky started clouding up and I overheard people talking about what Israel might do next. They are all frightened, Mama. Terribly frightened. And then on the way home, it started to rain lightly. It's amazing how things can change in such a short time. Even the sky senses it."

"I think you're letting your imagination run away with you. It's getting to be late in the afternoon. Why don't you make yourself a sandwich and then take a nap? I don't expect your father to be home until late tonight and we won't need to have a big supper, or any supper at all for that matter. You need some rest."

Liyah nodded and hugged her mom again. She made herself a Falafel, stuffing the pita pocket with mashed chickpeas, lettuce, tomatoes, cucumber slices, and spiced tahini sauce, then headed into the den to catch up on any news while she ate.

Forty-five minutes later, depressed by the repetitive bad news, Liyah turned off the television, dropped her empty dish and glass of half-finished milk in the sink, and headed up the stairs.

In her room, she sat down at the small desk next to the window. Every day she marveled at the lovely purple top with pink swirl-like clouds painted across its length, and its delicately turned legs resting on cat's paws. Her mind drifted back to when she was a little girl. Her dad had renovated this poor neglected piece of furniture, creating something amazing just for her. She had believed it was the most special thing in her life. *It still was.* A work of art, always there waiting for her. He had told her the delicate beauty and colors symbolized the iris, the flower of hope. She brushed her fingers across its surface. *It was a one-of-a-kind thing in the whole entire world*, she mused, *…and only hers.*

She sat down in her chair, flipped open her laptop, and waited for the screen to come alive, then clicked on the WhatsApp icon. Up popped two messages: one from a recent new friend she had met the last time she visited Esty at her home in Israel, and one from Zack, her friend from America, Detroit to be exact, who had been so important to her the past year. Liyah felt she gained a kind of physical strength from him, a *strength of being* she had never known. With him, along with Kai Li and Morningstar, they had helped change the course of events in Palestine and Israel that day, about half a year ago. It had been awhile since he last contacted her. She missed him and had been thinking about him when she was at the market, the same market she and Morningstar also visited during that time. She smiled. *He must have received my thought waves. Isn't that how it works? Like magic!*

She clicked on the message from Zack.

> Hi Liyah! Just checking in. I've seen on the news there's trouble near you. I hope everyone's ok???
>
> Have you heard from Kai Li or Morningstar? I've been tied up on a few things…also lazy I guess, too…haha! Sorry about that. I have something I wanted to ask you…about my dad. You're good at talking about things like this.
>
> Anyway, maybe we can have a call sometime?
>
> Zack

Liyah typed back:

Hi. Sure thing, Zack. Let me know what works for you.

Keep in mind the 7-hour difference between here and Detroit. Like you say, there's some bad stuff happening here, but I can be pretty flexible since my school has temporarily closed until some of this blows over.

Luv Ya...L

Liyah's eyes were beginning to sag. The day already seemed long. She took off her shoes and crawled underneath the blanket on her bed. *Maybe a quick nap to pick up her energy,* she thought. She closed her eyes. As she began to drift off, she thought she heard the muffled sound of explosions.

FOUR

IT WAS 4 p.m. on Sunday but Jerusalem was still alive with activity. Esty Blum had completed the last of her usual afternoon tours through East Jerusalem, covering the holy sites of Christian, Jewish, and Islamic religions: the Church of the Holy Sepulchre, the Wailing Wall, and the Al-Aqsa Mosque (home of the Dome of the Rock).

She exited the Old City wall via the Jaffa Gate and wove through the bustling crowd, making her way along the street to the parking lot. Her dad always let her use his car to get to Jerusalem and back for these tours—only about a mile and a half from their home in Talbiya. On weekdays, after school, he would pick her up and bring her home. But on weekends, Esty had the car to herself since he would usually be settled in at home, reading.

The unmistakable sound of the click of a fob released the driver-side latch as Esty neared the car. She opened the door and flung her backpack into the passenger seat. It was a warm day, low eighties, not unusual for Jerusalem this time of year. She removed her cellphone from the side pocket of the bright blue blazer that sported the Israeli Tourism Ministry emblem stitched to the left breast pocket. She folded her jacket, placing it neatly on top of the backpack. Her blue puffy newsboy cap followed, releasing the long blond hair that had been imprisoned inside it during the tours. Esty then slipped behind the wheel of the year-old BMW, it's interior still holding the smell of new car upholstery.

Before pushing the dash button to start the car she typed her code into the phone keypad; no new text messages, but two voicemail messages: one from her dad, and the other from Hanna, her closest friend growing up. Hanna's family, the Coopermans, had moved to a kibbutz in southern Israel a few years ago, a little less than two hours from Jerusalem, but they were forever friends and were in constant touch. She clicked on her dad first.

"Esty, it's Dad. I've been called in to meet with the Prime Minister and Cabinet about the recent developments I mentioned to you last night. Looks like it will last well into the evening. I had to take a taxi in and can take one back home tonight…whenever that's going to be, so don't wait up and don't worry about me. Make something nice for dinner for yourself. And for me of course…haha! I'll get it from the fridge later.

See you in the morning, sweetie."

Esty clicked on the next call. She heard the sound of nothing at first except strange noises, like firecrackers in the distance. Finally a voice, hushed and panting, breaking up in intervals.

"Esty…call your dad…tried emergency…can't get through. Can't find my parents… they came to pick me up yesterday at the festival…I was taken by some people in something like an army Jeep…guns, killing…awful. Spent last night in a building somewhere in Gaza City. I hid my phone. Don't know where they're taking me today. Just broke free but …Oh God! Here they come!…Get help Esty! I…" She heard the sound of the popping of gunfire, then nothing.

"Hanna! Hanna!" Esty screamed before realizing she was shouting at the voicemail. Her mouth hung open and a chill ran through her body.

Esty stared at the phone, then she spun her head around to see if maybe something might be happening there, too. But she caught herself. *How stupid is that, Esty? Get ahold of yourself!*

She checked the time of the message: an hour ago. She sat back in her seat catching her breath, trying to think of what to do next. She wouldn't be able to get hold of her dad, but what could he do anyway? Calling the emergency line would be useless since Hanna was in Gaza. Her fingers fumbled as she tried to locate Hanna's contact info. She pressed on the home number.

The call went to voicemail.

"Mrs. Cooperman. It's Esty," she said, sitting with her back straight, trying to control the panic in her voice. "I got a call from Hanna. She's in trouble in Gaza…but you probably know that. Please call me as soon as you can."

Esty sat back again against the headrest. *What now?*

She glanced at the time on her phone again, then blankly out the windshield. *What festival was Hanna talking about? Was it the one nearby Re'im where she lived? Probably. But hadn't it ended? If I wasn't so busy yesterday and today maybe I'd know more. Was this part of the trouble her dad had mentioned?*

It would take her only ninety minutes to get to Hanna's home in southern Israel, in the Negev, if she pushed it, she thought. Someone must know something there. "But what about Gaza?" she whispered out loud.

Esty started the car and pulled out of the parking lot. Her house was only a short distance away, so she stopped by, made some sandwiches—leaving one for her dad—exchanged her blazer and khakis for a light jacket and jeans, stuffed some other clothes and supplies in her oversized backpack, grabbed several bottles of water, then dashed to the car and drove off, heading south.

It was 6:30 by the time she arrived in Re'im. Still no further word from either Hanna or her parents. Esty used the GPS to locate the Cooperman's home, parked the silver BMW in the driveway, and walked up to the front door. She rang the doorbell several times, peering into the hallway and front room. No one came to the door and there seemed to be no activity in the house. She went back down the walkway to the car, then drove slowly down the quiet street, past a couple of well-maintained modest homes until she came upon someone walking their dog across the street. She stopped, opening the car window.

"Excuse me. Hello! Excuse me, please. Can you tell me how to get to the festival?

The woman approached the car. "Oh, I don't think you want to go there," she cautioned. "The emergency vehicles, guards, and now the IDF are all over the place after the massacre."

"Massacre?"

"Where've you been child? It's all over the news. Everywhere!" She studied Esty. "I saw you pull out of the Cooperman's."

"Yes, I'm a friend of the family and am trying to find them."

"Sorry, I haven't seen any activity over there for the past two days. I'm hoping they're away and weren't part of the festival…you know, the Supernova thing they call a rave. Mostly young people. I don't really approve of things like that…all that partying and such. I…"

"Yes, well that must be it," Esty interrupted, her level of anxiety rising. "I know a little bit about it. Supposed to be a nice weeklong event with dancing. They call it a journey of unity, peace, and love."

"Uh-huh, whatever you say dear," the woman replied, a bit stiffly. "But like I said. I don't think you want to go there. You probably won't get past the guards anyway."

"I have to try," Esty replied, her words taking on a gentler tone.

"Well, okay then dear." She pointed in the direction to the right of where she was standing. "Just go out to the main road and take a right. It's up about a couple of miles off the road. You won't be able to miss it. Be careful."

Esty waved a thank you, then raised the car window.

As she approached the location of the festival, the level of activity increased dramatically. Many cars were on both sides of the road, some appearing abandoned. People were milling about, some leaving, and some walking toward the scene but off to the side of the road. As she got closer, she was stopped by a guard standing in front of a makeshift gate. She put down her window.

"Can I help you?" asked the man, standing ridged in full camo, wearing a helmet, a combat vest with pouches stuffed with ammunition, and carrying a large rifle. A Glock 19 was strapped to his side.

He glanced at the Government of Israel emblem affixed to the inside of the windshield.

"Yes, sir. I would like to see if I can find someone to help me. I had a friend who attended this event and both she and her parents can't seem to be located."

"That's unfortunate, but you have to have a pass to go any farther. It's really bad. Only soldiers, emergency crews, and government vehicles allowed." Esty followed his eyes as he looked over at the insignia on the windshield again, then back at her.

"Just a minute please, officer…ah sir." She opened the glove box and retrieved a piece of paper, handing it to the man.

He quickly scanned the document and studied the signatures and embossed stamp at the bottom, then brought his eyes back to Esty.

"You're a little young, aren't you?"

"What do you mean?"

"I mean you're a little young to be driving around in a car with a high-level government sticker on it." His voice was monotone and serious. "A little young in general I'd say. License please."

Esty pulled her purse out of the backpack, retrieved the license, and handed it over. He looked it over briefly then passed it back.

"I'm the daughter of…"

"Raise the gate!" the guard shouted to the other guards, before stepping aside and signaling her through.

Esty entered the site of the festival, driving as close as she could to the main stage area where the musicians had performed before pulling the car off to the side and stepping out. The sun was still above the horizon in the pale blue sky, but clouds were moving in. The temperature was already down in the 70s. Esty leaned back into the car and retrieved her light zip-up jacket just in case.

Emergency vehicles were still rushing in and out of the scene, picking up new bodies of the dead, while a host of military personnel stood guard around her. She could see even more posted throughout the scattered trees nearby that created the only shade on hot days.

Esty made her way toward what was left of the makeshift stage area, its high roof made simply of multicolored sections of puffy synthetic parachute-like material—many parts now partially dethatched and flying loose, others missing entirely. The picnic tables in the vicinity were vacant, with water bottles and cups scattered on top and underneath. Between the tables and toward the woods, she could see more trash along with pieces of clothing left behind in the rush to get away. Nearby and all around the area were cars abandoned by the dead and those fleeing the scene as they ran for their lives. Some of the cars had been blown up by missiles or grenades, and many were riddled with bullet holes. She could see some bodies still lying close to the cars, not having been removed yet since the military and some rescuers took almost half a day to respond. More were still arriving to pick up the remaining bodies and search for more.

The air didn't smell like fall in the desert to Esty but rather took on the mild stench of newly decomposing flesh. She had been to bombing scenes before in her short life—places where the dead had been trapped under the debris of buildings destroyed by missiles, as searches worked for weeks to find any signs of life. She knew that this odor would get worse over the next few days if the bodies weren't fully removed.

Esty suddenly felt light-headed. The thought of Hanna potentially being caught up in something very sinister, trapped somewhere all alone. Her mind sent her back in time, to a trip the two of them went on when they were only eleven, with their parents in Italy. It was spring in the Dolomites, and her father had arranged a special ski holiday. They stayed in a small private villa a short distance from the family-friendly Val Gardena resort. It was very private and had its own small skating pond in the back. Early one evening, after dinner, she and Hanna donned their skates. They moved along the ice on the pond, pretending to be world-famous skaters in the Olympics.

The ice was soft from a warmer than usual spring, and thin in places. She remembered hearing a loud crack, and in seconds the ice gave way under her. She fell through the ice and into the frigid dark water. When she tried to come to the surface her head hit the ice above. She remembered panicking, and swatting at the ice, knowing she was about to die…then nothing after that.

Hanna's dad had been watching and told her later that Hanna dove into the water to get her. Hanna was able to eventually free her but then was caught herself, trapped under the same ice. It took him a few minutes to get to them. Esty recalled finally coming to when her dad dragged Hanna out of the pond. Hanna had stopped breathing and had to be resuscitated by her dad and then taken to the hospital. She knew Hanna had risked her life that day to save her. It had all come back in a rush.

Esty sat down on the end of one of the picnic benches under the canopy to steady herself. She was the only one there. Everyone else was either searching the wooded area, investigating the hundreds of cars that remained along the road and in the parking areas, or part of the emergency response teams milling about. An eerie silence enveloped her, interrupted now and then only by a brief gust of desert wind or the distant voices of rescue workers.

She fingered the silver pendant on the chain around her neck. It always gave her comfort in the months since the trouble in Jerusalem and reminded her of Ahmad and Liyah. Liyah had given both her and Ahmad a similar pendant as a present the last time they were all together with her other new friends Zack, Kai Li, and Morningstar on the Mount of Olives. Hers was one half of a silver heart, with an *A* hand scratched by Liyah on the back. Ahmad had the other half, an *E* scratched on his. She missed all of them, but at least had Liyah and Ahmad nearby in Gaza.

Esty held the pendant firmly in her palm and felt its energy. She had been able to see Liyah several times since then. During those times Liyah passed on some of her knowledge about the magic-like power of the pendants, knowledge passed on to her and the others by Ooray, the mystical being whom they had seen once at the Temple Mount in Jerusalem when they helped save the Old City and prevent an even wider spread catastrophe in the Middle East, and then again at the Mount of Olives before everyone left. She had some experience now in the use of these things to create strong magnetic fields, and even start fires or protect those around her.

She remembered the scene in Jerusalem when they used these powers to protect the city. It was there, too, that Ooray became an eagle and brought everyone in the square into the past, recounting the thousands of years of history in only minutes for that entire region—the Lavant, and describing the chain of events over those millennia that would connect Liyah and Esty, Ahmad and her other new friends, and Jews, Christians, and Muslims to their common beliefs, sources of strength, and shared humanity.

Esty clutched the pendant tightly in her hand as she thought of her friend. Her eyes filled with tears. *Where are you?*

She focused her attention on Hanna and began to see vague images of people shouting and the sound of explosions and gunfire. The visions suddenly became clearer, and a movie started running through her mind as she looked out across the landscape.

A missile or rocket-propelled grenade suddenly landed nearby with a thunderous explosion. Bodies flew into the air. People from the stage were screaming and pointing toward the fields surrounding the event. Dozens of men and boys approached rapidly from different directions in pickup trucks and motorbikes, some now even jumping from the vehicles and running. They fired their machine guns and automatic rifles into the crowd.

People screamed and tried to get away. They were shot down before they could gather their belongings. Some ran to their cars but were chased down and mercilessly executed as they opened the car doors.

As the movie proceeded, people were dragged from their cars and either shot or carried away in the trucks and on the bikes. The entire event lasted for over twenty minutes, but Esty saw the movie in only two, in true Technicolor.

As it wound down, Esty witnessed Hanna being forced into the cab of a truck at the edge of the wooded area. Then at the end, she saw a picture of Hanna tied up and sitting in a narrow passage that looked like the underground tunnel that Ahmad described when he searched for Liyah's kidnapped brother, Khalib.

Esty brought her attention back to the current moment, letting go of the pendant. She gazed around at the scene once more. It was calm. Only the devastation and debris of the attack remained, along with the smell. The military guards and others were still canvassing the area. Her eyes landed on a group of policemen standing by a car in the parking area a short distance away. She made her way towards them.

"What can we do for you, young lady? This isn't a place you should be," one of the men said as she approached. "I'm Captain Haviv."

"I have a pass in my car, sir. The guards let me through. I'm trying to find out where a friend of mine and perhaps her parents might be."

"I'm afraid you'll have to wait until we check all the hospitals and the reports that the emergency teams and guards, and IDF are compiling. It could take weeks…maybe even longer."

Esty caught a glimpse of the driver's door of a white sedan behind the officer. The window was smashed, and the side panels of the car were filled with bullet holes, except for the space in the middle, streaked with blood stains from where a person had obviously been standing.

The officer turned around to see what she was looking at, then spoke again bringing her out of her stupor.

"If you give us her name and your number, we can keep you advised as we find out more."

"Sorry…ah, yes…so, her name is Hanna," she finally replied, shaken. "Hanna Cooperman. Her parents are Noah and Abigail." She pulled her phone from the pocket of her jeans as the officer finished writing down the names. She held the screen with her address in front of him. "And here is my number."

After adding it to the other information on his clipboard, he looked up. "I'll be sure to let you know if we hear anything, Ms. Blum. Nice to meet you. Please stay safe. It appears you are quite a ways from home…and it's getting late."

Esty nodded and forced a smile. "Thank you, Officer Haviv."

She turned and headed back to her car. The sun was touching the tops of the trees. She opened the door, slid behind the wheel, and gazed out of the windshield watching the last rays of the red desert sun as it descended below the tree line.

FIVE

DEEP IN SLUMBER, Liyah's mind stepped back in time. Back to when she was a little girl trapped in her home. Militants had tried to kill her father by throwing a bomb into their home as he led his family to shelter.

Her body twitched as she revisited the moments when the bomb exploded in the living room as they made their way down the stairs to the basement of the house. The militants were finally cleared from the street and an emergency team rushed her parents and her brother to the hospital. But they didn't notice *her*, buried beneath chunks of plaster in a side room. She woke up under debris, panicking and choking on cement dust, feeling like she would suffocate at any moment.

"Baba! Baba!" Liyah called out desperately for her father, but no one was there to hear her. It was all too real again. She was all alone and no one was going to find her.

Her body stirred as her dream of the past ended. She lingered in a state of semi-consciousness, as her mind shifted to a new dream. In this new story, she was again trapped underneath rubble, from a missile attack. A heavy ceiling beam, crushing the life out of her, suddenly turns into a wooden bookshelf, pressing down on her back. She was no longer at her home in Beit Lahia. She remembers she is in a café in Gaza City, begging for help once more. This time calling out Morningstar's name. But no sound was coming out of her mouth. "*This is all too real to be a dream, isn't it?*" she heard herself say. "*Am I back there again?*"

She begins to fade deeper again. She lets go and follows this new story her mind is weaving, concocting a new ending to that old incident with Morningstar.

A beam of light makes its way through a hole in the debris heaped on top of the bookshelf, sneaking past an opening in the frame and finding Liyah's left eye. She blinks twice and breathes heavily, fighting back the fear. The light transforms the molecules of her body into a narrow stream, allowing them to escape upward inside the light. Up, up the milky stream travels, through the broken window of the café and out into the sky above Gaza. Higher and higher the stream of atoms rises, at light speed, escaping the pull of earth's gravity and piercing the dark vacuum of the galaxy.

Her very essence of being then reassembles itself in a cabin in some unfamiliar location. She was sitting on a sofa. Flames shoot up from the logs in a fireplace across from her, and a strange multicolored prism of light vibrates, making itself visible above the mantle.

"Ooray?" she whispered.

"Yes, Liyah." Replies the ghostly form in a voice indistinguishable between male and female.

"What is happening?"

"You were calling me."

"I was?"

"Well, you were thinking of me. Even if you didn't know it. We are always connected, remember?"

"I think so. Yes. I remember this place now. It's where I met Morningstar, Zack, and Kai Li."

"Yes, it is."

"Why? Why have you brought me here?"

"So you will remember."

"Remember?"

"Remember that you are no longer afraid of anything. That you made it through the explosion with your family and the time you were saved by Morningstar, and when you in turn saved her in the cave that day along this journey. Do you remember there is nothing in your world to be afraid of? Why has fear returned, Liyah?"

Liyah studied the light, trying to find something new about it, about Ooray. "I, uh. Well, I think it must be the bombs."

"Bombs?"

"Yes. I heard some explosions. They reminded me of being trapped. It seems that fear never goes away."

"Perhaps not completely, Liyah. But it is only a shadow of itself. And if you were awake you would not be afraid. Because you have already proven that."

"Awake? Am I dreaming?"

Ooray laughed. "Are you?"

"I don't know. But I do know that I am sorry that I let you down."

"Nonsense. You have done nothing of the kind."

"I have not been true to the mission. I have not worked hard enough the last few months to pass the knowledge I have…the gifts you gave us…the light."

"It takes time, Liyah. You cannot do it alone."

"But maybe this recent thing, the massacre by my people of the Jews in the Negev near where I live. Maybe it wouldn't have happened if I…if I had just done a little more."

"It would have happened anyway, Liyah, because those are not your people. No more than the extremists in Israel represent Esty or her father. Extremists on either side are not real Jews or Palestinians. They don't want peace, they want power. They are terrorists and bullies who act out of a deep sense of fear and cowardice.

"But you are right to refocus your energy on the mission. Your friends feel the same way, you just don't know it. They are becoming anxious, too. They see the times are getting more troubled, but they know they will be ready to help you…as you are ready at any time to help them. You all know that.

"You have already touched so many, Liyah…Esty, Ahmad, your brother Khalib, your parents, Yusuf the falcon trainer, the people in the square in the Old City when Jerusalem stood at the crossroads…"

"It was you in Jerusalem, Ooray."

"Yes, I was there, too. For you. You called me. But no one would have been there if it wasn't for you. It didn't require special powers for you to bring them all together. Only yourself, your love for them, and your commitment. The deep compassion that makes you, you. That is the glue…your magic."

Liyah sighed. "Sometimes, Ooray, I think I don't know what's happening. What's real and what isn't? Now is one of those times. Not only here but back at home. I believe I have these powers and yet at times I feel powerless. I don't know what you expect of me…I'm only one person."

"You are right, the powers you have come to know cannot solve all problems, and you cannot be everywhere at all times. Neither can your friends. But together you can, you and all the others you touch who in turn become powerful unto themselves…and who pass their strength to others.

"The powers you and your friends have come to possess cannot change everything. And a single power will not save your world. Nor will the power of religious or political leaders. Leadership is often corrupted by money and self-interest—the opposing forces of true leadership…because the ego makes people blind. Do you remember this from before?"

"Yes," she said softly.

"Real leaders have a role to play, but in the end, the transformation must begin at the bottom, with each person, and become a groundswell. The force will come from the collective consciousness, the sum of the enlightenment of all, and from their overt actions in passing the light until it leaves no one out. At that point, when there will be no space left for those who abuse power and hurt others, everyone will be safe, and happy…at last."

"I fear, though, that this new trouble where I live will once again paralyze progress in our land and destroy the good we have already accomplished."

"I have been this way before, Liyah. And it's not only me, but also others like me, and those we have shared the light with, as you are now doing. There will be setbacks. The vacuum of the darkness is a void that has a long history, just as the fear in mankind has a long history as well. It is our job to shine the light into that void until all the darkness and fear are exposed and overcome."

Liyah felt herself buoyed, but at the same time overwhelmed. Proud yet uncertain of her ability to live up to the promise she made to Ooray and her friends that day less than a year ago. Tears welled up in her eyes and she felt a lump in her throat.

"What if I fail?"

"You will never fail if you follow your heart and put others first, Liyah. Sometimes the timing is off, not yours but the world's. Jesus, Muhammad, Moses and so many people throughout history have shared this light with others, yet the world was not ready. But their light, yours, and the light of others like yourself always continues to shine and multiply. It all counts. It adds toward the collective total…and will triumph in the end."

Liyah's body stirred once more. Lying on her side, she opened her eyes and stared at the wall next to her. *Was this a dream?* She wondered again. "Or was I with Ooray?" She closed her eyes and snuggled back under the covers.

Six

ESTY WOKE TO the sound of massive explosions that shook the building and almost tossed her out of bed. Blinding flashes of light lit up the window next to her. She jumped to her feet, stunned, as much from not knowing where she was as by the sound waves rattling the walls of the room.

Hugging the wall to the side of the window, afraid it would burst into pieces at any moment, she glanced out. Capturing a brief glimpse of the devastated buildings only a couple of blocks away, she ducked back. The room was dimly lit, but the partially clouded sky told her it was morning.

Esty waited until it seemed like the explosions had ended before making her way to the wall outside of the bathroom and flicking on the switch. She put on her jeans, sneakers, shirt, and jacket, grabbed her phone, purse, and room key, and headed down the hall toward the red exit sign. She remembered she was in a hotel but not the name of it. And she knew she was on the 4th floor. She took the stairs, not wanting to get stuck in an elevator if any bombs should hit the building or cut off the electricity, finally arriving at the front desk.

"Hello, young lady, how can I help you?" asked the male receptionist, staring at Esty, caught by her long blond hair and blue eyes. A rare sight.

"I was wondering if my car would be safe here," she replied. "I parked it in the garage underneath the building, but I will be out and about today and didn't want to drive it…that is, given what's been happening. If you know what I mean."

"I certainly do. And yes, we have a guard who watches over the grounds and the parking areas."

"Okay, great. And where might I get some breakfast?"

He pointed to his right. "About halfway down that corridor there you'll take your first left. You can't miss the sign."

She made her way to the restaurant and took a seat in a small booth, away from the other patrons. An elderly waiter handed her a menu and poured her a glass of water.

"Juice?"

"Yes. Please," answered Esty.

"I'll be right back for your order."

Esty removed her phone from her jacket pocket and checked for any messages from Hanna, but there was nothing from her either in voicemail or by text. But there was one text from her dad, saying he received her message when he got home late the previous evening and she should call him. The phone indicated the text came in at 10:30 p.m. The current time was 9:50 a.m. She pressed his name in her contact list.

"Hello, sweetie. Are you on another one of your adventures? I think if your mother was alive she wouldn't be happy about you being in Gaza, with what is going on now."

"Sorry, Abba. I got a call from my friend Hanna. She seemed to be in trouble. So, since you said you'd be late, I thought I'd take a quick trip down there to see her."

"Quick trip? To Re'im? At the Ministry today we were briefed about the trouble there.

Esty was silent. Pictures of the festival site flashed in her head. She had pushed them out of her mind until that moment.

"Esty?"

"Yes Abba, I'm here. Sorry. I saw the festival site. I can't talk about it right now, only to say there were plenty of police and guards everywhere."

"Did you stay at Hanna's house?

"Uh, not exactly."

"Not exactly? What does *that* mean? Are we getting ourselves in trouble again?"

Esty sensed an unusual tightness in his tone. "Is everything all right?"

"You should come home right away, Esty. I'm worried about how this is all going to go. The detailed plans for a response are being kept secret and handled by the IDF and the Prime Minister. But there will be a swift retaliation, you can be certain of that. I just don't know exactly when or…"

"It's already happening, Abba. I heard some explosions this morning."

"What? Where? Where are you?"

"Uh, I'm, well, in Beit Lahia with Liyah," she lied. "It was late and it's only a short distance across the border from Re'im to her place. The explosions were in Jabalia."

"Why didn't you just stay with Hanna?"

"I think Hanna has been taken as a hostage. I overheard some guards talking about people being taken somewhere. Sorry, I'll try to get home tonight. Will you be okay without the car?"

Esty waited during a long pause, hoping her father wasn't going to chew her out until she couldn't stand the silence. "Abba?"

"I'm here, sweetie. That's terrible! I don't know what to say. It's not your fault, and I'm fine without the car. I can call for a ride in, or even walk if the weather stays good. It's you I'm worried about. This could escalate quickly and you might get stuck there."

The waitress approached the booth. "Can I take your order?" she asked, pencil and pad in hand.

Esty glanced up at her and spoke haltingly into the phone.

"Um, I'll be fine Abba. And I'll be home shortly. Gotta go. Love you!"

"Order?" her father questioned. "Esty, are you there?"

Seven

ESTY GOT DRESSED after brushing her teeth and taking a much-needed shower. She drew the curtains open, plunked herself down in the chair next to her bed, and stared out the window at the smoke rising from a number of buildings only a few blocks away. She could even see the rubble from the damage of the explosions at the intersection of some of the streets. Pillars of smoke still rose from what appeared to be a ten-block area. *Must have been missiles,* she thought. *A lot of them.*

The dampened sounds of sirens from ambulances, police cars, and other vehicles seeped through the walls and windows of the hotel, becoming an incessant drone to her ears.

She felt the weight of the situation and questioned her decisions. *What could she have done to help her friend? What the hell was she thinking after all? Was she going to find Hanna somehow in one of those underground tunnels? What hospital would they have taken her parents to? Maybe they'd be at the morgue…but where? Or was it that she subconsciously knew she needed to see Liyah?*

She picked up her phone from the desktop next to her and clicked Liyah's number, then waited.

"Hey Esty! What's up?" came the excited voice on the other end. "I've been missing you …was just about to call you myself."

A broad smile painted over the serious expression holding Esty's face captive. "Hi Liyah! Yeah, it's been too long. I guess a few months."

"Well, it's great to hear from you. Anything special?"

Esty took in a deep breath, letting it out slowly to calm her anxious nerves. "Yeah, well, have you heard about what's happened the last couple of days?"

"You mean the attacks by Hamas?"

"Yes, well certainly that. But I guess I mean the explosions in Jabalia early this morning?"

"How did you know about those already?" asked Liyah, clearly surprised. "Are they already in the news in Israel where you are?

"I heard them."

"Heard them? What do you mean?"

"I'm here, Liyah. In Gaza."

"Here?"

Esty sighed. "It's a long story. I have my dad's car and it might be hard to get out of here, even with his pass. And with the Israeli sticker on the windshield, I really shouldn't stay where I am."

"Where exactly?"

"I'm at a small hotel in Jabalia."

"Allah! Really? Then you're probably only a couple of kilometers from the house. There's a room waiting for you. Well, my room anyway." She chuckled.

"I promised my dad I'd be back in Jerusalem later today, and I have more tours in Jerusalem I have to conduct this week."

"Can't you stay at least one night? Please, please, please."

Esty hesitated. "I don't think so, but we'll see."

"Well, come over right away so we can catch up."

"I want to check out the hospital here first, Liyah. The desk clerk told me it's called the Al-Amal International Hospital…biggest one in the area close to the border where all the trouble occurred. It's the most likely one in Gaza where I might find Hanna or her parents…unless her parents were taken to a hospital in Israel. But that would be much farther away from Re'im."

"Re'im? Hanna? Oh Allah! Allah! What do you mean Esty? Is everyone okay?"

"Sorry. That's why I said it was a long story. The short answer is I don't know anything more, except Hanna was kidnapped from the peace festival in Re'im and I can't locate her parents. I got a panicked voicemail message from Hanna then nothing after. That's basically why I'm here."

"Let me help. What can I do?"

"Nothing at the moment. Really. I'll check out the hospital and then get back to you. Okay?"

"Sure Esty. But be careful. And if you get in a jam and don't have your phone, then think of me…you know what I mean? Just think of me and I'll be there."

"Yeah, I get it." Esty laughed, grabbing hold of the half-heart necklace around her neck that Liyah had given her, its other half to Ahmad. "I've got your address. See you shortly."

Esty pulled her zip jacket from the closet, wrapped it around her waist, and donned her black hijab. She then slung her backpack over one shoulder and headed out of the room and back down the hall.

Arriving at the front desk, she tapped her palm on the button of the stainless-steel bell on the counter. The receptionist made his way from the adjacent room.

"May I help you?"

"You may," replied Esty, wearing a warm smile. "Can you tell me where the Al-Amal International Hospital is? I can't seem to locate it on my GPS inside this building."

"Sure." He pointed to the street across from the main entrance. "Just go through those doors and take a right. It's about five blocks up. But be careful. There's a lot of commotion everywhere out there, especially near the hospital due to the missile strikes. The injured are being taken there. And be careful, too, not to take a left out of the main doors, because that will bring you straight to the market in the refugee camp…that's where the missiles landed." He brought his eyes to Esty's. "They tell me it's awful. Just horrific!"

She nodded. "Thank you, sir."

Esty made her way through the main doors to the street and followed his instructions, leaving her car in the garage. The whine of distant sirens filled her ears, unprotected now by the walls of the hotel. A light smokey smell drifted through the air. As she approached the hospital the activity around her became more frenzied. Police cars surrounded the area and ambulances rushed in and out of the emergency entrance.

Esty hustled up the stone steps, pushing her way past the heavy metal doors, and approached one of the information desks in the reception area. A woman at the counter in a white hijab stared into the computer screen, as doctors and nurses shuffled to and fro down the hallway. Visitors packed into the elevators to check on injured loved ones brought to safety from the attack on the refugee camp.

"Excuse me."

No response.

Esty cleared her throat loudly. "Madam?"

The middle-aged woman looked up over her glasses that rested on the end of her nose. "May I assist you, young lady?"

"Yes. I'm looking for someone who may have come here the other day…from the attacks in Israel…Re'im to be exact."

"We don't get many people here from across the border. Most of them make the longer trip to Israeli hospitals further north. But, given the seriousness of the injuries and large number of people, we did actually get some. What is the name?"

"Cooperman. Hanna Cooperman. And also her parents…same last name."

The woman's fingers flashed along the keyboard. They stopped as her eyes scanned the screen. She looked back at Esty. "No…Sorry. No Cooperman on the list here."

Esty frowned. "Okay. Well, thank you. I guess I'll try the police station and visit the other hospitals in Gaza."

"I doubt you'll have much success. There's no telling which station might have been involved, if at all. And it's a mob scene in the streets due to the bombing of the refugee center. It would take you a lot of time to check the hospitals in person."

Esty stared out the large window near the entrance, taking in the growing frenzy of activity outside, wondering what to do next.

The receptionist waited until she returned her attention. "I'll tell you what. I have access to the registers of patients and staff at all the hospitals in the area. Let me check for you." Her fingers once again danced over the keys until a new screen came up. She scanned it, then repeated the sequence a number of times, finally stopping after a few minutes and returning her attention to Esty.

"Sorry. I don't see anything at any of the hospitals in the area. No Coopermans."

"I see," Esty replied. "Thanks anyway. I appreciate it."

"It doesn't mean they aren't there," the woman said, taking in the glum expression on Esty's face. "Just that it's unlikely."

"Yes. Well, thanks again."

Esty made her way back through the main doors and out into the warming morning air. She slipped the backpack from her shoulder and sat down on the first bench near the front of the hospital, then gazed into the near distance, toward the once sprawling refugee camp. Pillars of smoke still rose from its streets, and the sounds of sirens were everywhere. She thought of her friend. And wept.

Eight

AHMAD STOOD BENT over the table in the main office of the production section of the Filastin Dawn, scrutinizing the final proof of a special afternoon edition. The massive presses whirred like a jet engine, still churning out extra copies of the morning paper. They rattled the large glass windows that separated rapidly spinning rollers from Ahmad and the office above.

Liyah's dad entered the room.

"How's it goin', Ahmad? How'd your article turn out?

Ahmad finished reading the last few lines and looked up. "Great, sir! At least I think so. Quite a rush putting it together."

"I imagine," replied his boss. "Between the Hamas attacks in Israel and now Israel's retaliatory strikes on the refugee camp, things are getting more than crazy. That's why we have to get out another edition even though there's still demand for the morning paper."

"Yes, sir. I know. But I'm more worried about where this is all headed. We were making such great progress after the previous attack on the Old City in Jerusalem a while ago. But now this!"

"Have you heard anything from your girlfriend?" his boss said, winking.

Ahmad's face flushed as he tensed his shoulders. "Ah, what do you mean?"

"Just pulling your leg. I mean Esty." He chuckled. "I have my sources you know…just like you."

"Sources?"

He laughed again. "Never mind, Ahmad. I was simply wondering if you heard anything from her about the views of Israelis, or even foreigners, whom she guides on the tours…something we might add to the articles."

Ahmad let his shoulders relax. He smiled. "Well, actually I called her a few times about that the last couple of days but haven't heard back."

"I'm sure you will," his boss replied, smiling back. "And, oh, do you still have contacts with anyone in Hamas or others you met when working on your first article? The one we published in the *Dawn* the day of the dinner at my place in Beit Lahia? Must have been close to six months ago already now."

"No. I haven't needed to. But I'll do some digging."

"That would be good, Ahmad. This recent missile strike was only a few miles away from here. That's way too close. And I don't know how bad it's going to get after that vicious attack by Hamas on the kibbutz across the border. Any info you can get could be critical."

"Yes, sir."

"Great. Thanks, Ahmad," his boss said, turning and heading toward the door. "And say hello to Esty for me."

Ahmad could hear him chuckling as he closed the door behind him.

A few minutes later his phone buzzed on the shelf next to him. He reached and picked it up.

"Esty?"

"Hi, Ahmad."

"Something wrong?" Ahmad replied, "You sound down."

"That attack on the refugee camp…it's close to the Dawn, isn't it? I wanted to make sure you were okay."

"Yeah, pretty close, but we're all fine here," Ahmad assured her before his tone turned slightly short. "I left some messages. Where've you been?"

"Sorry. A lot's been going on. Remember my friend Hanna? The one who lives in the Kibbutz in southern Israel? Well, that's the one in Re'im and she was at the festival, and I can't locate her. And then the guards were everywhere. And now this in Jabalia. And…"

"Holy Crap, Esty. Take a breath! How did you hear about that attack? It was early this morning. Not that long ago?"

"I heard the explosions from my hotel room."

"What? What do you mean you *heard* them from the hotel room? Where are you?"

"I'm in Jabalia."

"What!?" Ahmad replied, incredulous.

"I went to look for Hanna at her home because I couldn't reach her. Then I ended up here because I got an interrupted voicemail message from her saying she was being held captive in Gaza."

"Seriously?"

"I wouldn't joke about something like this, Ahmad."

He paused a moment to process the information. "So, where are you now?"

"Sitting on a bench near the Al-Amal International Hospital. I thought perhaps she or her parents could be there."

"Her parents?"

"It's a long story. I got ahold of Liyah and I'm planning to spend the night at her place. But I miss you so much. Can you meet me there after you finish work?"

Ahmad shifted his attention from his own situation to his love for Esty. He knew he had adored her from first sight, and while the distance between her home and his was a blockade of sorts, they had called each other almost every day since then. And during the few times they had seen each other over the last six months, when Esty visited Gaza, he felt they both knew the early infatuation had turned quickly to feelings of real love. His voice softened. "I miss you, too. But I don't know when I'll be out of here. It's real busy and we're trying to get another edition out."

"Well, text me when you know for sure. I'll see what Liyah and her family's plans are when I get there. Hope I can see you. If not, then perhaps tomorrow?"

"I'll make the time somehow, Esty. For sure."

"Love you, Ahmad."

"Love you, Babe.'

Nine

ESTY GOT UP from the bench, slid both straps of the pack over her shoulders, and made her way in the direction of the smoke. She could feel the late morning sun on her face. Soon, winter would arrive, but for now, the last gasp of fall warmth kissed her skin and brightened her day.

The main road headed toward the refugee camp was busy. People stopped and shopped at the small stands jutting out from in front of the building along the way. Brightly colored banners hung overhead, the same ones used to block the blistering sun on summer days. The street was alive, buyers and vendors buzzing about, bartering, haggling over prices. Once in a while they would point toward the camp and wave their hands in anger, shouting something in Arabic that Esty couldn't understand, or stop and stare as an ambulance, lights flashing and siren yelping, forced its way back up the crowded street to the hospital.

In less than a mile, Esty neared a police barricade, blocking all traffic except emergency vehicles. She looked up at the sky. The sun was trying to fight through the gathering dust from the blasts that drifted into the streets and alleyways. An eerie orange haze filtered the light as it tried to make it to her eyes.

She continued her way along the sidewalk, past the last policeman standing at the end of the line of yellow sawhorses.

"Hey! You!" shouted the officer.

Esty turned to face him as she kept on walking.

"You don't want to go any closer," the man added. "It's dangerous over there."

"I'll be fine, sir!" Esty shouted back.

The officer held his arms out to his side, palms up, shrugging, as if questioning her sanity.

A short distance further she turned to her left, following a side street toward the center of the pillars of smoke. Three more blocks up she entered the outer edge of the of the damaged buildings. Chunks of cement littered the sidewalk along with collections of broken glass from the windows of the buildings, blown out by the concussions of the explosions.

She turned the corner ahead, stopped in her tracks, and stared up the street. Her unbelieving eyes captured the scene: the street was littered with the remains of several buildings—obliterated entirely. Heaps of shattered, unbaked sandstone bricks were piled high where the buildings once stood, along with sections of cement beams, their iron rebar rods sticking out the ends like arrows piercing the bodies of dead soldiers.

Rescuers climbed along the surface of the rubble, searching for any signs of remaining life. Heavy particles of dust now filled her nostrils, and she could hear the sound of emergency vehicles nearby, unable to get even close to the scene. Esty gazed upward once more, unable to see the sun, only more clouds of black smoke. The surreal scene numbed her mind. *Maybe I'm having a hallucination?* she wondered. She blinked several times then gathered her thoughts. *No. This was indeed real, and each of those black clouds above her was a scene like this.*

Esty removed her backpack and unzipped the main compartment. Reaching inside, she felt around, finally pulling out a soft, black-and-white keffiyeh. It was the one she had worn many times over the past year, when she visited sites after bombings, to help Palestinians, to visit the children and people in hospitals, to offer what aid she could. There had been a long lull in the bombing since the last time Liyah was there with Zack and Kai Li when Jerusalem had been saved.

But she knew something evil was again upon the people here, upon her.

She coughed lightly as she wrapped the cotton scarf around her neck, over her head, and across her nose and mouth, flinging the loose end back over her shoulder. *At least now she could screen out the dust that swirled about her.*

She donned her pack again and climbed the mountain of debris until she approached a young man, bending over and throwing chunks of heavy plaster to the side, then poking the pile again, as if hoping to locate a live body underneath an avalanche. Pulling the edge of the keffiyeh below her mouth she addressed him.

"Excuse me, sir. Can you tell me how all this happened?"

When the young man turned and faced her, she realized he couldn't be much older than her brother, Khalib. He studied her.

"Happened?" he replied, his tone filled with a mix of anger and sarcasm. "Where have you been? Damned Israelis, that's how. Missiles! Must be hundreds of people in this area alone…dead! No telling how many injured."

Esty stood in silence, lost for words.

"What are you doin' here, anyway? Not a place for someone like you."

"Me?" Esty replied, finally finding her voice. "I'm here to help if I can."

The boy appeared surprised, even stricken. "Help? What is it you can do? What can anybody do?"

"Where is everyone being taken?"

"If not the morgue, then to any hospital in Gaza City that has a spare bed. They're already filling up the Al-Amal International I hear. And the flow is constant."

"I heard this is because of the killings at the kibbutzim across the border."

"That's what *they* say, but I don't believe anything these days. Maybe they were staged."

"They weren't," Esty replied, flatly.

The boy studied her again. "How do you know?"

"I was there. I saw the result. And, besides, it's all over the news now."

"You were there? That's impossible. How did you get into Israel?"

Esty straightened her posture, locking her eyes on his.

"I *came* from Israel."

The boy paused, struck by her confidence and forcefulness.

"I have a few connections," she continued. "I saw the result of what Hamas did. Babies were slaughtered that day, women raped, men tortured and sliced to ribbons, and hundreds taken captive. Some people may be cheering in the streets because they are sick of the situation here in Gaza." She shook her head. "But I can tell you one thing…That was the face of pure evil."

Esty grabbed the end of the keffiyeh and held it up before him. "And we Palestinians are not evil. Hamas is not *us!*"

"You don't look Palestinian to me," the boy replied, studying her. "But there is something familiar about you. Like I've seen you before."

"The day is coming," she continued. "The day is coming when this will all end. We all need to be strong. Be our true selves. And know that the good people of Gaza and Israel will overcome the extremist leaders who use us as cannon fodder, forgetting the history of love here in the Levant, in Judea, in Palestine…in Israel.

"Thank you for your service," Esty said to him, before turning and walking away.

The boy's eyes followed her as she walked back down the mound of debris and into the street below until she finally disappeared into the crowd.

Ten

ESTY ARRIVED BACK at the Al-Amal International Hospital. She pushed through the heavy main doors and walked up to the same receptionist she had spoken with earlier.

"Well, you look familiar," the woman said, smiling at her.

Esty returned the smile.

"I have to say the keffiyeh looks good on you, even if it covers up that beautiful blond hair of yours." She winked. "I recognized you by your pretty face and those white running shoes."

Esty nodded.

"What brings you back so soon? Need some directions?"

"Yes, actually," Esty replied. "To the children's ICU."

The receptionist looked perplexed.

"There are some special kids I want to say hello to," said Esty.

"I see. I thought you were still looking for your friend and her family. I didn't know you knew anyone else here. Take the elevator to the fifth floor and follow the signs. You'll find the ICU halfway down the main hallway…on the right. But don't be surprised if they don't let visitors in. The floors are getting overwhelmed by the flood of new patients, especially the ICUs."

Esty turned and made her way to the bank of elevators a short distance away. Above a set of swinging doors on the fifth floor, she noticed the sign for the children's intensive care unit. Passing by it, she found the first bathroom on the same side of the hall, opened the door, and then locked it behind her. She placed the backpack on the toilet and pulled out a rolled-up black leather trench coat from the bottom of the main pouch. Taking out a checkbook and pen from a side pouch she scribbled something on the top check, folded it into the front pocket of her jeans, and returned the pen and checkbook to their previous location.

She put on the coat with its large black buttons, tied the leather sash around her waist, and pulled the broad-winged collar up around her neck. After placing the backpack behind the toilet tank, she fixed the edges of the keffiyeh tight across her chin and down over her forehead. Turning the knob on the door she entered the hall again, then pressed her hand against the right side of the swinging doors of the ICU.

She stared blankly, unnoticed, wondering if she had suddenly left her past world behind the swinging doors and entered into a version of *Dante's Inferno*, where instead of the villains paying for the vices of man's nature it was the innocent who paid: those who were still too young to have accepted any justification to hurt another being, too inexperienced—uncaptured by the ways of the world, of the long trail of history's human cruelty to one another.

Absent was the pained cheering of the patched and hurting adults in the hospital she had visited last spring in Gaza. *Here is an even sadder scene,* she thought, *if there could ever be such a thing. Little lambs, suffering in silence.*

She listened intently, her ears picking up an eerie silence, broken only by the high-pitched beeps of the myriad of monitors spread throughout a vast open room, and loudish whispers of reassurances, hushed into the ears of each child by vigilant nurses.

A nurse, close by, wearing scrubs and a surgical cap, was speaking to a doctor in a white hospital jacket, a stethoscope hung around each of their necks. The nurse held a clipboard in one hand, scanning it with her pen and apparently checking off a list of items as the doctor spoke hurriedly, pointing to several beds nearby and various pieces of medical equipment.

She scanned the room again, estimating the number of beds to be maybe fifty or sixty, with about ten or twelve staff members frenetically tending to the children, constantly monitoring their condition, which for most appeared extremely serious. A few of them seemed to be sleeping or drugged, but the faces of most of those she could see still wore grimaces of pain.

She took a step closer to the doctor and the nurse, still unnoticed by either, or anyone else in the room. Their voices became clearer. The doctor was questioning the nurse about the status of several pieces of equipment and informing her of the plan to add additional beds in the already overcrowded room, and reorganizing them so the children with the more massive injuries would be together at the far side of the room, behind screens, and getting the best of attention and the equipment the hospital could give.

"They are still coming in," the nurse lamented. "Even with additional beds, we will be running out of them. And equipment will have to be shared if at all possible."

"We've requested emergency support from hospitals close to Gaza City," the doctor replied. "Linens, medical supplies, beds, IVs, feeding tubes, catheters, ventilators, syringes…everything possible."

The child in the bed nearest them moaned. The nurse reached out to hold her hand and whispered something in her ear before turning her attention back to the doctor.

"Five children died already this morning. Sadly, it frees up beds for us to take in more who might stand a chance. But the flow is too much. We're losing the battle."

"I know, Risha. I know."

The nurse placed the pen at the top of the clipboard and turned to move to the next bed.

"Allah! Nura!" she gasped, dropping the clipboard, which fell onto the floor with a loud *Whap!* and catching the attention of all the nurses, doctors, and other members of the medical staff. They focused their attention on the girl in the black trench coat, the white and black keffiyeh—

symbolizing the homeland of the Palestinians—and the white running shoes.

Gasps of "*Nura!*" then filled the room, drowning out electronic beeps from the equipment and silencing all the voices.

Nura searched the large open floor, nodding to the staff. She pulled her keffiyeh down below her lips so she could speak freely.

"Thank you for your service," she said loudly, clearly, slowly. "The world would be nothing without *you.*"

She glanced around the room again, resting her eyes briefly on each staff member, before continuing. "I have visited many hospitals in the past two years. But I have not seen anything like this. So many children. So much pain. May Allah bless all of you for what you do. You are angels, living on earth among us mere mortals."

"No!" Shouted a nurse from across the room. "It is you, Nura. You are the one sent to help us all. To give us hope. That is how I see it!"

"Yes!" a few others shouted in support, along with a burst of applause from all the staff.

As the staff turned quickly back to the critical things at hand, Nura nodded again to them, then stepped closer to the doctor and nurse she had been listening to. She shook their hands.

"I don't want to disturb things here. I know you are so incredibly busy. I happened to be in the area. I saw the destruction at the refugee camp and was told most of the severely injured were being sent here. I just wanted to see the children and thank all of you."

"Thank you too, Nura," the doctor replied. "Come with me."

He walked her around the room, stopping at each bed. Many of the children had thick white bandages wrapped around their heads, hiding the large gashes and sections of fractured skulls. Some were missing an arm or leg. A few had lost several appendages. They ranged in age from about one to sixteen. The staff tended to faces and bodies that had been sliced by shards of glass and crushed by chunks of cement. They treated broken bones, changed dressings, and set patches covering injured eyes, or to the socket where an eye had been. They were constantly cleaning wounds, stitching new ones, gently removing bandages that stuck to the ooze of bodies trying to overcome life-threatening burns, checking the IVs and monitors, and moving back and forth between beds helping the children. Helping each other, hour after hour. Never ending. Exhausted.

The doctor then brought Nura through a set of hanging, wide plastic strips at the far side of the room, and into the neonatal intensive care unit.

"There are so many children that are coming in," he explained, "we had to move those under a year or two old here, where we normally care for only those babies who were born preterm or just born and need special care. But to free up beds in the ICU, we took more kids under the age of two and created makeshift beds here. That's why it's so crowded. We can barely squeeze between them."

Nura looked down at some of the premature babies struggling for life in what appeared to her to be incubators of a sort. She kneeled down next to one of the small beds where a little boy, maybe a year and a half old—his full body and head bandaged, looked up at her. All Nura could see were his brown eyes, cheeks, pudgy little nose, and tiny mouth.

"His name is Sameer," said the doctor.

"Hello, Sameer," Nura said, her voice quiet, gentle, loving.

The little boy blinked several times, then raised his bandaged arm to her. As Nura touched her index finger to his cheek, his tiny fingers wrapped around it, weakly at first, then squeezing tighter, like he was never going to let go.

Tears poured out of Nura's eyes and flooded down her cheeks. She took her other hand and caressed the side of his head, then bent closer and kissed his forehead. He smiled.

The doctor placed his hand on Nura's shoulder. "I know," he said. "It's beautiful and sad all at the same time."

Finally obtaining Sameer's permission to stand up, she faced the doctor.

"I have to go."

"We are thankful for your visit, Nura. Every Palestinian knows your name. We are lucky to see you…to have you here."

"I am the lucky one, doctor. There is more strength and love in this room than anywhere else in the world at this moment. It fills me up and renews me."

She shook his hand one last time. "Thank you for your good works. Please thank the entire staff."

"Certainly," he replied, leading her out of the NICU through a side door. "If you take your first left up there you will come back into the hallway where the main entrance to the ICU is."

Nura nodded, thanked him one last time, and made her way to the bathroom. After a few minutes, she re-entered the hallway wearing a zip jacket and carrying her blue backpack over one shoulder.

The elevator doors in the lobby opened and she made her way past the growing line at the front desk, serviced by several receptionists. She stopped at the end of the counter and waited until she caught the eye of the receptionist she had spoken with before. The woman held up her index finger to the person she was assisting and walked over.

"Hello again. Did you find the children you were looking for?"

"Yes, thank you so much." She reached into the pocket of her jeans and retrieved the folded check. "I want you to take this to the director of the hospital. It has the name of a woman on it…an E. Blum. But the account is good and so is the signature mark, even if appears a bit like a scribble."

"Sure. Happy to do it. Anything else?"

"No, but thank you for everything."

Esty turned, walked across the foyer to the main doors, and disappeared into the crowd on the street.

As the receptionist returned to help the visitor, she unfolded the check; made out for 20,000 US Dollars to the Al-Amal Hospital.

Eleven

LIYAH WAS SITTING at the head of the table in the dining room when her mother returned from the kitchen after drying the last of the sandwich plates. She stood at the other end of the table, watching her daughter, slouched over her cell phone and tapping away.

"You need to get a life, Habibti. What have you got planned for the rest of the afternoon?"

Liyah stopped typing with her thumbs and looked up. "Not much, since school is closed and people are afraid to go to the market after the missile attack in Jabalia this morning. And that was Esty texting me, anyway. She says she'll be here shortly."

"I wish you'd given me more notice about her visit. I don't have much time to get something special for us for dinner."

"No worries, Mama. I didn't get much notice myself. She's part of the family now. I doubt she wants you to put yourself out."

"Well…"

"Seriously, Mama. She'll be happy with anything…and besides, she says she has to get back home as soon as possible."

Her mother left the room, passed through the front hall, and started up the stairs. Halfway up she was almost knocked down as Khalib flew down the stairs, taking two at a time, and brushing against her against the banister.

"Khalib! Allah! You tryin' to kill your mother?"

"Sorry, Mama," he grunted, jumping the last two steps and landing on the wood floor in the foyer. He entered the kitchen, pulled open the refrigerator door with gusto, and fumbled around. Finally removing a large tuna wrap his mother had made for him, he snatched a half-liter pitcher of orange juice, set the wrap on the plate she had just washed, and joined Liyah in the dining room.

"What's up, Liyah? I hear Esty is coming here today. Been a while, hasn't it?"

"A couple of months at least."

Khalib took a huge bite of the sandwich and started talking as he chomped away at it. "I'd be surprised if she gets past the border guards after all that's happening. Did you know that Israel declared war on Hamas? Not a great time to choose to come here, I'd say."

"I think she was already in Gaza when Israel made that statement…and please…don't talk with your mouth full. It's gross. No one wants to see that. I hope you don't do that when Esty's here."

"She's hot! You don't have to worry about that. Best behavior."

"And don't ogle her like you did the time we all had dinner together with her and her dad. It's embarrassing. You're like a dog with its tongue hanging out."

Khalib laughed.

"Are you headed somewhere?" she asked, her expression softening a bit.

Khalib took another bite and a huge swill of orange juice straight out of the pitcher.

Liyah frowned. "Allah, Khalib. Really?"

"I'm gonna catch up with some friends at the square. Before we're all under attack and hiding in our basements."

Square. Liyah's thoughts suddenly jumped back to the previous spring when her brother was abducted by terrorists, and the ensuing rescue mission involving her, Morningstar and the others, and her new friend at the time: Esty. They had found him right before being taken across the border toward

Syria. It seemed like an age ago. She remembered how worried she was for him. How she missed her younger brother and fought to obtain his release. And then when Khalib helped all of them, including Ahmad, Zack, and Kai Li fight off the drone and missile attacks in the Old City.

She studied her little brother. He was two years younger than she was. He was staring down at the phone in his hand, flipping through the apps with one hand, devouring the sandwich with the other. *Boys. Would she ever understand them? Especially this one…barely fifteen years old and caught between puberty and the demands to become a man…too soon. How could she ever forget how much she missed him those days he was held captive by terrorists? She feared for his life. But how proud she was of him, too. How she cared so for him.*

She reached over and took his hand from the phone, holding it softly in hers. "I love you, Khalib," she said. "I didn't mean to jump on you. Tell me you will be careful. That you'll stay safe. I could never survive again what happened in the spring…thinking you were gone forever. Lost in the tunnels, then being taken out of the country."

Khalib put down the sandwich, grinned, and rested his other hand on hers.

"What's up, sis? We just made a *sandwich* with our hands. I promise not to take a bite." He chuckled but kept his eyes locked on hers. "You goin' sappy on me?"

She smiled and pulled her hand from between his two. "Oh, stop it! We seemed to be making at least some progress in the last six months. Not enough, but some. And not just you and me. I mean with making gains like Ooray wants us to do. To lead others. To share the light…*you* know. To change things here in our homeland once and for all."

Khalib downshifted his tone, now appearing more reflective, sober. "Yeah, I do know."

"It wasn't a dream, Khalib. It's all very real. The change can come if we build the foundation with others. Ooray said one day when the world is finally ready, it will happen in a flash."

"I believe that, Liyah. But I feel I haven't been active enough, until recently, when Hamas attacked the kibbutz. The missile strikes kind of knocked me back into orbit. I've been talking to some kids my age the last few days, sharing what really went on in the Old City that day. People forget easily or discount the *magical* part of it all. I don't blame them. Sometimes even I think it was a dream."

Liyah scanned her brother's face. She could sense his concern and sincerity. "Yes, I feel that way from time to time. But I am certain more than ever about the mission Ooray sent me, Zack, Morningstar, and Kai Li on, and now you and the others. It's been a little difficult with me and Esty because she is so far away. She doesn't get here much and it's hard for me to get to Jerusalem."

"It's going to be even harder now that war has been declared," Khalib cautioned.

The *buzz* from the front doorbell interrupted them.

"Will someone get that?" her mother yelled down the stairwell.

Liyah let go of Khalib and stood up. "Got it, Mama!" She unlatched the door and opened it.

"Remember me?" Esty joked, sporting a wide grin.

"Esty!" Liyah screamed. "I got distracted and almost forgot you were on your way."

As soon as Esty stepped across the threshold, she dropped her backpack and the two fell into each other's arms, unable to curb their excitement.

Esty finally pulled free. "I'll have to stay at least one night maybe more if that's okay. But I'm concerned about the car. It has the Prime Minister's seal on the windshield and I fear something will happen to it."

"Don't worry. The driveway is private and the hedges and olive trees will help hide it. And I told you, you can stay as long as you like. We've got a lot to catch up on. It's been a couple of months, hasn't it? "

"Yeah, it has," Esty returned.

"Well, come on in. We can set things up in one of the rooms later. Khalib's anxious to see you," she winked at Esty. "I'm sure."

"Where is he?"

"Right here, Esty." Khalib blurted out, entering the hall. "I saw that wink. Someday you won't be able to make fun of me. I'm already taller than you." He grinned like the Cheshire Cat, then laughed.

"*Some day*?" Esty questioned, scanning him from head to toe. "I'd say you're just about there. Did you grow six inches since I saw you last? And so handsome."

"Okay," Khalib replied. "I guess after that I'll have to let you get away with it…this time."

Liyah led them past the dining room and into the den. Khalib took his dad's recliner, while his sister and Esty sat in the two wing-back chairs across from him.

"What have you been up to, Esty?" asked Khalib. "Kind of a tough time to be visiting Gaza. How'd you get through the checkpoints.?"

"I came in last night, over by Beit Hanoun. The security was already strict by that time, but my dad has those special passes that get him about anywhere he wants to go. I carry a letter in the glovebox in addition to the Ministry seal on it that explains I am his daughter. But it might be more difficult to get back into Israel now. War was declared after I was already here."

Esty continued, explaining about Hanna and her parents, the shameless disrespect for lives at the Re'im festival, the devastation at the refugee camp, and her visit to the hospital. She glanced at Khalib, who had managed to morph his lips from a smile to a frown. "You okay?" she asked. "I'm sorry for going into such gross detail on the horrible things I learned about Re'im and the suffering I witnessed at the hospital of all those innocent kids caught in the missile strikes on the refugee camp."

"Sorry," replied Khalib, his eyes focusing riveted to hers. "Some of the boys I know, even a few of my friends, reacted to the news about the attack on the Re'im festival by sort of celebrating, cheering, and supporting those who took part in it. Not me, and not my best friends. I've been talking to them about…you know, about what you both taught all of us: how everyone in the old Levant—Jews, Muslims, and Christians all come from the same early communities, shared the land for thousands of years, and the common spiritual values of all their religions." He glanced over at his sister.

Liyah smiled at him. "Glad to hear that you're making an effort to teach others what you picked up from us, Khalib. We need you to help influence those your age. It is sad though, that so many are using that terrible event to spew hatred."

"Yeah. It is," he replied. "But most all our lives we have been told stories about how Israel is taking our lands illegally and controlling our lives. How we all struggle every day, with a boot on our necks, unable to stand up. With little to no hope left. Hamas says they are fighting for our rights to survive when no one else will."

A quiet stillness captured the room for a moment, finally broken by Esty, but in a soft voice.

"Nothing, excuses what happened in Re'im, Khalib."

"No one in any universe can think that is okay," added Liyah, clenching her teeth and tightening the muscles in her neck. "Or much worse…take joy in it!"

"I know, I know," Khalib replied," his voice urgent. "That's not how I feel. I'm not defending them. I'm aware of how the media pukes out a lot of propaganda all the time, basically pumping us full of crap and hate, 'till we're near bursting. It's not me…I'm just saying I see how this hate seems to have been here forever and keeps growing with each act of suffocation upon us Palestinians."

"I'm sorry," Liyah replied. "I didn't mean to sound angry with you. Just the situation."

Khalib's face cast a weary look. "Well, it's likely to get even worse around here now that Israel wants a war."

Esty's phone vibrated in her pocket. She took it out and checked the screen. Holding up her finger, she whispered to the others. "It's Ahmad. I'll be right back."

They watched as she disappeared down the hall, excitedly chatting to Ahmad, finally hearing the front door open and close.

Outside, sitting on the stoop, Esty held the phone in her lap and pressed the speaker button.

"…so like I was saying. It's just too crazy here. I won't be able to get there tonight. Can't you stay longer?"

"I may have to…but only for a few days. I have to do something to try to find Hanna."

"Sounds like a long shot."

"I know, but I have to try. I'm just afraid to call my dad and tell him."

"I bet. Well, look. Why don't you see if Liyah can invite me to breakfast there tomorrow? I can stop by before work, but I hate to invite myself by asking her dad. Know what I mean?"

"I'll see what I can do. I'll text you later."

"Great Esty. Can't wait to see you."

"I hope so." Esty paused briefly. "Doesn't really sound it."

"Oh, c'mon now. I'm under a lot of pressure."

"All right. I know. I didn't mean it, Ahmad."

"I know, sweetie. Bye for now."

Esty ended the call and made her way back in and to the den.

"Where's Khalib?" she asked Liyah.

"He went to his room. Said he wanted to make a few calls."

"I hope he isn't pissed. Kind of a depressing conversation."

"He'll be fine. How is Ahmad?"

"Okay, I guess. Not seeing him much lately makes me upset. And now this situation is keeping us apart, even though I'm in his backyard. He asked me if he could stop by in the early morning before work. Would that be okay?"

Liyah's thoughts drifted for an instant, to when she saw Esty and Ahmad sneak a kiss the night of the celebration six months ago. She'd been caught by surprise, thinking there was perhaps some chance *she* might be the one. She'd never even suspected it was Esty. *But why would he even have thought you cared,* her mind whispered to her. *You never showed your cards.*

She reeled in jealousy for a brief moment, then hugged Esty tightly realizing how much she loved them both.

"Yeah. For sure, Esty. I'll make it happen."

Twelve

THE SUN WAS sinking lower in the bright afternoon sky of Gaza City when Ahmad strode under the banner bearing the image of a falcon and into the Café Saker. He spotted a balding, middle-aged man with a full black beard wearing an olive green Taqiyah hat, sitting by himself in the far corner. As he neared him, the man stood up and reached out to him.

"Ahmad! *As-salaam-alaikum*."

"*Wa-alaikum-salam*," Ahmad replied, shaking his hand.

"Can I get you an espresso?" the man offered.

"No. I'm fine. Thanks anyway."

"What brings you out of your lair at the Filastin Dawn?"

Ahmad grinned. "Trying to get stories as usual."

"You mean probe me for dirt?"

Ahmad laughed. "Well, not unless you're dishing it out. No. I'm concerned about what's happening, as we all are. There have already been two sets of missile attacks, mostly closer to the Dawn than here. I'm looking for your perspective on those and the attacks across the border at Re'im. I appreciated your contribution to my very first headline story in the Dawn, after the attacks on the Old City during the holy days last spring. You have a long history with Hamas and are well connected to many of the leaders."

"Ah. Indeed. History, yes. But no longer an officer. Retired early you might say. Trying to make a living running a fish store in town here. I thought it would be less dangerous…but apparently not. Things are getting out of control, wouldn't you agree?"

Ahmad sat back in his chair and stared directly into Malik's eyes, something he had learned to do when speaking with highly mistrustful people or someone like Malik—aspiring to be a good person but linked to evil men. "Yes…That's why I'm here. I have two basic questions. I promise to quote you as an *inside source* without using your name…as usual."

Malik sipped his demi-tasse of espresso and set it gently on its saucer. "Shoot, my friend."

"First, why was it necessary to attack the Israelis so brutally?"

"It was necessary to get their full attention. To show we are fed up. We can't breathe here in Gaza and they continue to take our lands in the West Bank…their slow but steady creep of settlements. They are hoping there will come a time soon when it will be too late for us. Besides, when some people are as angry as that things can get out of hand."

Ahmad straightened his curly dark hair across his forehead and leaned forward, his dark eyes still connected to a matching set across from him. "*Out of hand*? Really? C'mon. I may be young but I'm not stupid. There are many ways to get their attention, Malik. That was pure evil and it was not just *a few* people. It was mass torture and murder without mercy against men, women, and children…by many men in multiple locations." He moved closer to Malik. "It was planned."

Malik blinked several times as Ahmad retreated in his seat, composing himself.

"I cannot counter your assessment. I simply don't know for sure. I guess I am grasping at straws, wishing it hadn't happened, and looking for reasons. It's why I moved out of the inner ranks a while ago. I see things as getting more radical. And when the Israelis double down as they are doing now by declaring war, I feel that this is what the extremists really want. On both sides."

"How do you mean?" Ahmad questioned.

"I mean we know that the Prime Minister of Israel has no intention of stopping the illegal settlements or working toward a two-state solution, providing a true home for all Palestinians. He has said so publicly. Why would we doubt him?

"The leaders of Hamas have always denied the right for Israel to exist and threatened to push the Jews into the sea. The more they can get the Israelis to react as they just have, the more Palestinians they get on their side. I think Hamas has led Israel into a trap, to incite other Muslim partners in the region, like Syria and Iran, to join in the fight."

"What happened to the majority of people on both sides wanting that ultimate peaceful solution?"

"You've got two extreme positions, both digging in and ratcheting up the stakes. Pretty soon it takes on its own life…and you get war. From my perspective, Hamas never really cared about a peaceful solution, or what is good for all Palestinians. They care about power. Same for Israel. It is about a few powerful people wanting even more power. They couldn't really give a crap about sharing or caring. It's about control."

Ahmad took a deep breath and let it out, allowing his shoulders to finally relax. "So, that gets to my second question. How do you see this all unfolding now? This *war*?"

"Frankly, not well."

"Like?"

"It's a war, Ahmad. Israel has already started blowing up sections of northern Gaza and announced their intent to invade with their troops. Not sure when that will happen, but I don't see them stopping there or even here in Gaza City. They'll go all the way south. To Rafah."

"But if Hamas releases the hostages what's the point?"

"No point at all, my friend. No logic involved here. The hostages are all Hamas really has, except for hand-to-hand combat in the overcrowded and crumbling cities. Both sides have now trapped themselves in a vortex of hate, and only Allah knows how it will end."

"It always blows over." Ahmad offered.

"This isn't a gust of wind, Ahmad. This is two tornados gaining strength, heading right for each other, sucking in everything and everyone around them."

Ahmad sat silently, fearing that what Malik had said was not as overblown as he might normally expect from a Hamas connection. But Malik had nothing to gain by hiding anything or exaggerating. The facts seemed to be clearly out there for all to see. *Maybe he is right,* Ahmad thought. *Was this to be the final storm, one of uncontrollable proportions, still growing, right here in his own backyard?*

Thirteen

LIYAH AND ESTY faced each other cross-legged on the floor in Liyah's bedroom, between Liyah's bed and the spare bed her father brought in for Esty. Their chatter was interrupted by a knock on the door.

"Good night, girls. It's late so don't stay up much longer, okay? You need your sleep."

"No worries, Mama," Liyah replied.

"Good night, Mrs. Rahim."

"Good night, dear. So nice to have you here."

Liyah smiled at Esty as her mother made her way down the hall. She let out a giggle like she remembered she used to do with her friends there in Beit Lahia when she was a little girl.

"So fun, Esty! I'm glad you made it here, even if it was under such dire circumstances."

"Me, too. But I've got to figure out what to do next to locate Hanna and her parents. I spoke with my dad while you were in the bathroom getting ready for bed, and he's not so happy. He's letting me stay a few more days since he doesn't really need the car, but he says things might be going downhill fast and I need to get home and out of Gaza while I still can."

"You can't blame him. People are getting really concerned. I think my mom's gonna have a stroke worrying about Baba when he's at work. The area near the Dawn has been bombed several times before. And the recent blasts in Jabalia at the refugee camp were not that far away."

"Did you check with your mom about him? Is it okay for tomorrow morning?"

"Who...? Oh, you mean Ahmad. You left me behind there."

Esty laughed. "Yeah, sorry. When you said 'Dawn' my mind drifted there."

"Yup. All set."

"Thanks. I told him I'd text him only if there was a problem. So, we'll likely see him first thing."

"What do you think you'll do about Hanna?"

"I'm hoping Ahmad might have some way of finding out through Hamas. It's a long shot, but I don't see any other way. I called Hanna's home number but there's still no answer. And I haven't had any luck at the few hospitals I tried. It's likely that she is still being held captive…no idea about her parents."

"This whole thing is just awful, Esty, isn't it? I wish I was able to do more to *pass the light* as Ooray puts it. Maybe it could have made a difference."

"I feel the same, but I think this freight train had already left the station and was headed here quite a while ago. I doubt we could have had any effect. Besides, didn't Ooray say it had to be done from the ground up and was going to take time? We only just started planting the seeds. Speaking of Ooray, have you heard from Morningstar lately, or anyone?"

"Well, the last time I heard from Morningstar or Kai Li was a couple of months ago. They both said they were stalled a bit…like you and me. They are talking to others and practicing with the gifts we all got from Ooray…you know, the bands and necklaces we showed you when we were all together in the Old City, but moving slower than they'd like. Zack sent me a note the other day, wanting to talk about his dad. I think I may have mentioned that. I should get back to him pretty soon. Before things heat up even more around here."

Esty began playing with the half-heart pendant around her neck. "I think I just feel, well…*stuck* too."

Liyah reached to her side and opened the drawer of the small table between the beds, retrieving the wristband and necklace that Ooray had given her the first time she met Morningstar, Zack, and Kai Li.

"Remember these?

"How could I forget?" Esty sighed. "I remember using them when we saved Khalib from the terrorists, and then on the Wall like you say. Fabulous gifts from Ooray. And very powerful."

"I noticed you playing with your half of the necklace you and Ahmad got last spring. It reminded me."

"I did have a question about those," Esty replied.

"What's that?"

"I've played a lot with this necklace you gave us. I can feel the strong energy in it when I cup it in my hand. But I can't seem to make things get set on fire like we did saving Khalib."

"The gifts we received from Ooray in the very beginning of our journey are more powerful than the ones we pass to others. They can focus the energy more if you aim your fingers, and even transport you to a new location, or even back in time.

But the ones we gave you and Ahmad still are very powerful. It's a matter of learning how to focus your mind. You can test its capabilities and limitations by practicing. I'm always finding out more about the Timeless Teardrop Necklace, and I use the bracelet to focus energy on protecting myself, moving objects, and things like that." She laughed. "Actually scares me now and then."

Esty laughed with her. "I see. Well, maybe we can practice together while I'm here?"

"Absolutely! One of the things Ooray pointed out to us is that in the long run, it's all about everybody finding their own gifts and using them to help others find the light within themselves, and the light of love and compassion…then, in turn, passing a piece of it on by helping others in the same way."

"Like a chain reaction," Esty added.

"Yeah, but scaling logarithmically, ultimately becoming a sort of explosion."

"I get it, Liyah. Thanks. I guess I'm just anxious to make a difference because the more I'm aware of this the more I also see more clearly all the darkness in the world. And that scares me."

"It's always been there, Esty. But that's our mission. To keep the light alive and pass it along to overcome the dark. Kinda like the firekeepers throughout human history…but maybe a final chance to save us all."

Fourteen

THERE WAS A rap on the door. Liyah's mother wiped her hands on her apron, made her way from the kitchen to the front hall, unlatched the door, and drew it open.

"Well, hello Ahmad. *Sabah al-khair.*"

Ahmad nodded. "Good morning to you, too, Mrs. Rahim."

"Come in. The girls are late, of course. Their father left for work an hour ago. He's working long hours these days."

Ahmad stepped across the threshold and into the hall, slipping off his dark blue denim jacket and hanging it on the coat tree next to the bureau. "I know. These aren't good times. I'll be joining him as soon as breakfast is over. Thanks for inviting me."

"Esty and Liyah would have sent me to see Allah if we hadn't." She laughed. "But don't get me wrong. We are honored to have you, young man. David thinks the world of you...I'm sure you know that."

Ahmad smiled. "Never hurts to hear it," he said as he tailed her into the dining room.

"Have a seat, Ahmad. I'll go get them."

At the top of the stairs, she knocked gently on Liyah's door and twisted the nob slowly, opening it a crack. "Let's go girls. There's someone downstairs waiting for...."

Esty flung the door open and blew past her, followed moments later by her daughter, moving at a slower pace.

Ahmad heard the thud of two feet landing solidly on the wooden hall floor. He turned to his side and stood up. Before he could slip away from his chair, Esty flew into his arms.

Liyah entered the hallway. A lump of jealously grew in her throat, even though she had witnessed their reaction to each other several times before. But perhaps the feeling was lessening in intensity each time. She hadn't realized in those earlier days, when she first met Ahmad, that the notion of him would grow in her quiet thoughts, sneaking up on her, until part of *him* would seem part of *her.*

But that was then, she mused. *And now is now. And how I love them both. Wasn't I the one who gave them their pendants?* She caught up to them, wrapping her arms around them in a group hug until they finally broke their grip and sat down at the table in front of the place settings that awaited them.

Liyah's mother readied the breakfast serving in the kitchen, rattling pots, opening and closing the oven door, and retrieving milk and juice from the refrigerator. The excited greeting chatter in the dining room subsided.

Ahmad poured a little olive oil from the small crystal decanter onto his small side plate, then reached across to the tray holding small bowls of green olives, almonds, and figs, along with a plate stacked high with triangular sections of pita bread. Selecting a few of each of the options he assembled them in groups on his plate, dragged one of the pita sections through a dish of hummus, and dabbed another into his olive oil. He devoured both pieces of pita bread in no time, then popping a couple of almonds in his mouth he glanced across to Liyah and Esty who had stopped talking and were just staring at him.

Ahmad's eyes grew wide. "What? What?" he said, loudly defensive.

"I think we're just marveling at your ability to shut us out and dive fully into the breakfast snacks," Esty offered.

"For me, it was the attention he put into arranging the items on his plate with such concentration…sort of like he might be setting type at the Dawn," Liyah added before they both broke out in laughter.

"I'm so happy you're enjoying yourselves at my expense," Ahmad scowled before a broad smile lit up his face.

"Well, you kids seem to be having a good time this early in the morning," Liyah's mom said, placing a hot shallow glass dish on the slatted wooden heat protector at the end of the table. She collected their plates, scooped up a baked piece of the food in the shape of an omelet for each, and handed them back. She then made a trip back to the kitchen, returning with pitchers of milk and orange juice. And then one last trip to fetch a large bowl filled with slices of watermelon.

Finally taking her seat beside Ahmad, she looked over at the empty chair next to her at the head of the table and addressed the others. "Liyah's dad wanted to be here with you all, but he's under a lot of stress given the current circumstances with the sudden collapse of Israeli and Palestinian relations…not to mention the resumption of missile attacks. Sorry to bring it up, but it's right there smack in our faces, isn't it?"

"Yes, it is," agreed Esty.

"Well, enjoy this food," Liyah added. "We are all lucky for it."

"*Bismillah*," said Ahmad, bowing his head.

Liyah's mom bowed her head in response. "Thank you, Ahmad."

"What does that mean?" Esty asked.

"In the name of Allah," Liyah replied. "Often said before meals…sort of like a grace."

"*Barukh atah Adonai, Eloheinu melekh ha'olam, borei minei mezonot*," Esty returned in Hebrew. "Blessed are you, Lord our God, who creates varieties of nourishment." She then placed a forkful of the hot food in her mouth. "Mmm!" She looked across at Liyah's mother. "Sensational! What is this, Mrs. Rahim?"

"Emshat."

"Wow! Super delicious."

Liyah's mom smiled. "Thank you, my dear. You're too generous."

"No, I mean it! What is it?"

"It's basically a cauliflower fritter," Liyah replied. "You mash chunks of the cauliflower together with eggs, onions, parsley, flour, and spices. It's a favorite here in Palestine, but my mom does a special thing that makes it better than anywhere in the world."

"Stop it, Liyah," her mother scolded.

"And what is the secret?" Esty asked.

"Instead of just frying them, she quick-turns them in the frying pan then bakes them. Deee-lish!"

Ahmad chuckled. "Nice to be appreciated, huh, Mrs. Rahim? But she's absolutely right!" He finished his large fritter in three bites and reached for a slice of watermelon.

"What's with the watermelon, Ahmad," Esty asked. "I've seen it a lot in East Jerusalem cafes and restaurants."

Ahmad swallowed the big bite he had chewed only once, then paused. Holding the slice still close to his mouth, ready for a return trip, he answered her as if the half-bitten slice was like a microphone. "Favorite around here. For most Palestinians that is." He took another bite.

"And it's good for you, important vitamins. And lots of potassium," Liyah's mother added."

Liyah smiled at her. "Yeah, sure Mama. But what's *more* important…" She winked at Esty, "is that it symbolizes the struggle against the occupation. Its colors match those of the Palestinian flag."

The sound of a series of muffled explosions interrupted their breakfast, gently rattling the windows. Worry replaced the smile on Liyah's face.

Ahmad set the fruitless rind on his plate. "Sounds like it's coming from Gaza City…maybe closer. I better get going. But first…Esty, you never finished telling me about Hanna and how you got here."

"I'm curious about that myself, dear," Liyah's mom added.

"Oh, okay. Well, to make a long story somewhat short…Hanna left a voicemail message for me. She had gone to that concert in Re'im, and her parents were supposed to pick her up. The message was broken up a bit but I could tell she was one of the ones that had been abducted by the Hamas terrorists and is probably being kept somewhere in the Strip. Maybe Gaza City, or perhaps to the south. I don't have any idea. I came to Gaza to look for her…and possibly her parents. They seem to be missing as well."

"Oh, Allah!" Liyah's mom replied. "That's awful. My daughter tells me nothing, of course." She gave Liyah a sideways glance. "How did you ever get past the border?"

"I've got my dad's car and some papers he and I use when we leave home. Israel has control of the borders and he has the Prime Minister's seal on the windshield since he's a consultant."

"Not a good thing to be sporting around in Gaza these days though, I'd say," Ahmad replied, half serious, half sarcastic.

"No kidding," Esty agreed. "But I didn't know all the details of the massacre at the time, and it's only been the last day or two that Israel started the missile strikes."

"That's why we're hiding her car here for the time being. It can still get her out of here, but driving around the Strip in it would be suicidal."

"You girls do seem to find trouble wherever you go together, don't you?"

"Oh, Uma…Please. Let's not go there."

"Sorry, dear. Just saying."

Liyah frowned at her mother.

Esty glanced over at Ahmad. "I think you're right, Ahmad. You best be going to the Dawn. I'm sure Liyah's dad could use your help, and I don't want to keep you here just for me. Although I would like that." She smiled warmly at him.

Liyah glanced at her friend and laughed. "Pretty soapy, Esty! We'll have plenty of time. You're stuck here for a while from what I can tell."

Ahmad stood up and excused himself from the table. "I hate to eat and run, Mrs. Rahim, but it looks like that's exactly what I am going to do. Thank you so much for a wonderful meal."

Liyah's mom rose and hugged him. "See you again soon, Ahmad. Don't be a stranger."

Esty and Liyah walked him to the door. Ahmad swung the door open and stepped outside.

"Oh, wait!" Esty blurted out, taking her phone from her pants pocket. "I almost forgot the most important part. I need help finding Hanna." She flipped through her photos, finally stopping on one. "Here's a picture of her."

Ahmad studied the girl with the brown hair twisted into long braids and stunning green eyes. "Okay. I'll see what I can find out from my side. Send it to me."

Esty clicked on the photo and then deftly thumbed the keys. "Done."

Fifteen

AHMAD SAT IN the small, open office area he shared with two other reporters, neither of whom were present. He was tapping away, hunched over his keyboard and oblivious to the bustling newspaper world around him.

"Ahmad," his boss called out, walking up behind him. "Ahmad!" he said more forcefully when he didn't answer, finally tapping him on his shoulder.

Ahmad jerked his head around, almost falling out of his chair.

"Sorry, sir." Ahmad apologized profusely. "I didn't hear you sneak up on me."

"Sneak up? I wouldn't call it exactly that."

"Oh, no, sir. Certainly not, Mr. Rahim. I didn't mean…"

"Relax, Ahmad. It's quite all right. I guess everyone is jumpy these days. You must be working on something important?"

"Well, sort of sir. I have some ideas for a new storyline, given the rise in extreme behavior on both sides."

"I see. That's good. I'll look forward to reviewing it. But I told you before, let's dispense with the 'sir' or 'Mr. Rahim.' David will do, okay?"

"Yes, okay, sir, I mean Mr. Rahim…I mean…David."

Liyah's dad grinned. "Perfect."

"Did you need me for something?"

"Yes. There's one thing in particular. I'm concerned about how close the bombing and missile strikes are. The Israelis seem intent on blasting the refugee camp to smithereens.

Maybe because they think a few Hamas leaders are hiding there. But regardless of why, this building is too close to their target, and I fear we may get caught up in the collateral damage."

"Not much we can do about that, except pray I guess," Ahmad replied.

"True. We can't move those huge, heavy presses anywhere. But we can move the smaller one into the basement just in case. Even if the building collapses, it's not very large and things in the basement could be protected."

"I'll get on it, Boss…David."

"Great. Thanks. Grab a few strong lads like yourself. You can move it in sections. Shouldn't take too long."

After David left the office, Ahmad checked the time on his phone, then pulled up Hanna's picture and called his Hamas contact again.

"Malik? It's Ahmad."

"Hello, Ahmad. Something urgent?"

"Yes. I'm sending you a picture now. Let me know when you have it up on your phone."

Ahmad tapped his fingers on the table until he finally heard Malik's voice again.

"Okay. Got it. Who's this?"

"Her name is Hanna. She's a close friend of my girlfriend, Esty."

"And…"

"And she is one of the people kidnapped during the raid on Re'im. Esty thinks she might be somewhere near here."

"Why would she think that?"

"Because there were hundreds taken from several communities and they would have likely come back through the holes cut in the border fences."

"But there were many attacks all along the border," Malik countered. "Half of them were far south of Gaza City, and Re'im is right in the middle. They could have easily transported her toward Rafah in the far south as up here."

"I suppose," Ahmad agreed, "but aren't there way more tunnels to hide them here than down south."

"I think you'd be surprised how many tunnels there actually are, my friend. Hundreds of miles. But you are right about there being more places to hide them up here."

Ahmad paused. "Well, I knew there were many, but not to that extent. How would we go about finding her?"

"Finding her? What do you mean 'we'?"

"Yeah, well you know what I mean. I'd keep your name out of it. It's a favor. And Esty's dad is well-connected to the Prime Minister. It would be looked at favorably."

"Tricky business, this," Malik replied, slowly emphasizing each word. "Both of us could lose our lives."

"You'd be safe, Malik. I'd be the one taking the risk."

"I don't see it that way. But I'll make a few inquiries and we can go from there. I'm going to do everything I can to stay out of this once I get some initial info. You'll be on your own after that. Got it?"

"Understood."

"Okay. I'll get back to you as soon as I can."

Ahmad was left with the silence on the other end. He pressed Esty's name in his contact list and waited.

"Hi, Ahmad."

"Hi, Esty. I'm in a hurry…can't talk much. I've got a lot of things to do for the paper, and a special thing for Liyah's dad. But I did call a contact about Hanna.

"Oh, great!" Esty replied, her voice overflowing with excitement.

"Well, we'll see. It's a long shot. And dangerous at best. Just in case, I'm transmitting the basic info for my contact to you now. Hold on."

Ahmad skipped to his contact list, copied Malik's name and phone number, and sent it to Esty.

"Check your email, Es."

After a brief pause, she replied. "Got it. What's his last name?"

"First name only. To protect the both of you. Don't share with anyone. And use only in an emergency, okay? That means if something happens to me."

"Don't even say that. Ahmad! If things calm down…"

"C'mon. that's not likely, is it?"

Esty didn't reply.

Ahmad took a deep breath. He sensed he could almost hear what she was thinking. "I'll keep you informed. Sorry, sweetie. I have a bad feeling about how this is all going to turn out here in Gaza. It feels different than any time before. We need to move quickly."

"I'm worried for you. For us. I didn't mean to drag you into this thing with Hanna."

He could hear her sniffling.

"Don't do that to yourself. Promise me you'll stay strong."

"I will," Esty replied, her voice barely audible and lacking the certainty he was looking for.

"Gotta go, Es. Stay safe. I'll get back as soon as I can. Love you."

Sixteen

IT WAS LATE afternoon. Liyah sat in front of the bureau in her room which doubled as a desk, making notes on a pad. Esty lay parked on Liyah's bed, the top of her body propped up by two pillows, her head against the wall.

"That's okay," Liyah spoke into her cell." No worries, sir. Thank you." She turned around to face her friend.

"More nothing?" asked Esty, sounding defeated.

"Sorry. That was the last one on my list."

"Well, thanks for calling. Besides the dozen hospitals I called between yesterday and today that makes over thirty-five—all the health facilities in the entire Strip. I appreciate your help. Only a few speak Hebrew, and the smaller ones, especially in the south, don't speak Hebrew or English much at all, so it was a big advantage to have you talk in Arabic when we needed it."

"Sorry Hanna or her parents weren't in any of them, Es."

"It's okay. It means they're probably still alive but being held somewhere. They say the hostages are likely split up all over the place…some in tunnels, mosques, homes, and maybe some in detention areas somewhere. I'm not sure her parents are even in the Strip at all, let alone Gaza City. The papers said a few people had escaped. They listed their names along with those who are now known to have been killed. Hanna is not on any of the lists. So, we can be pretty certain Hanna is here: in Gaza City or somewhere farther to the south. We just don't know where."

"Isn't that what Ahmad's contact is finding out?"

Esty smiled weakly at Liyah. "Maybe. Although I'm afraid we're gonna run out of time. My father's been patient, but I know I'll be hearing from him in the next day or two…to call me home."

Liyah walked over to the side of the bed and took Esty's hand in hers. "Look, we've been through so much before. We'll figure this out, too. You'll see. And if you have to go home, Ahmad and I will find her."

Esty smiled up at her. "Don't know what I'd do without you, Liyah. Our lives have changed so much in such a short time. All of us—Ahmad, Khalib, our parents...and other people we have touched so far. Ooray was right: we can make a difference. We only have to persevere. That's everything, right?"

"Yeah. Along with the messages of the light," Liyah assured her.

"But it seems at times the world is going backward, doesn't it?"

"No, it doesn't, Es." Liyah's words were clear and strong. "Be sure of that. It's all part of the plan. It will make us stronger. We mustn't fail, my friend…We will *not* fail."

Esty stood up and hugged her. "I don't want to be a downer, Liyah. I'm just still afraid at times."

"I used to have conversations like this with Zack, Morningstar, and Kai Li when we first met about a year ago," Liyah replied. "We build off each other, balance each other's strengths and weaknesses. I'll tell you what…grab your necklace and let's have some fun. I've learned a few things."

Esty slid her necklace over her head and held it out in her palm and Liyah retrieved her necklace and special bracelet from the drawer from the bureau. They sat side by side on the edge of the bed.

"Squeeze your necklace, Esty, while I do the same to mine, and hold up your other hand, palm facing me."

Esty obliged. Then Liyah held her own palm a few inches away. "Now, watch the space between our hands as I concentrate on transferring my energy to you."

As Liyah closed her eyes and focused her thoughts, a dim white light appeared in the gap between their palms. The light slowly but steadily grew brighter, then began to pulsate like the beacon from a ship flashing signals to another. Liyah opened her eyes and watched as Esty became transfixed on what was happening.

Liyah reached out and gently rested her other hand on Esty's knee. "Keep your eyes on the light. I'm going to think of infrared light, the frequency visible in a laser. I learned about this kind of light from Kai Li. He used it for communicating with the drones when they were used to swarm airfields last spring and fly with the falcons in the Old City. He told me humans can only see this light at a certain frequency, but that it can be used to carry a lot of information…and heat when highly focused."

Esty glanced at Liyah who seemed almost in a trance, then followed Liyah's eyes back to the gap.

The flickering white light turned red and became a steady beam. The beam began to fade in brightness, but as it did Esty began to feel a warm sensation in the center of her palm, radiating outward. Liyah cupped her fingers to focus the light. As her fingers came closer together the beam disappeared. But seconds later Esty hastily yanked her hand away.

"Ouch!"

"Sorry. I got a little carried away. I don't have perfect control over things as you can tell."

Esty smiled. "Well, it wasn't that bad. I guess I was more surprised than anything. How did you do that?"

"It takes time to play with all the options…like brightness, frequency, intensity, color, an all that. I just wanted to give you an example of how light energy can be transformed into heat energy. I've been working on a few things like this to try to understand more of the capabilities and limits. Zack is ahead of me on this, I'm pretty sure. Don't know about Morningstar." She held out the bracelet. "You can do most of the same type of thing with this."

"Do you remember how we saved Khalib that day last spring when we found him in the underground cavern beneath the remnants of the ancient Anim Synagogue, on the way to the Jordanian Border?"

"Of course," Esty replied, taking the bracelet in her other hand. "How could I ever forget? I used it like you taught me, to concentrate its energy by focusing my attention on it like you just did and pointing my hand at the ground. White light streamed from my fingertips and set the grass on fire, and we used the smoke from the fire to force the kidnappers out of their lair…along with Khalib."

"Exactly. And then again at the Old City when we countered the missile and drone attack. White light, if concentrated enough, like when you use a magnifying glass to focus sunlight, can create heat, like the infrared light."

"Yeah, but we used the necklaces more, didn't we?

"We used both," Liyah replied. "And by holding hands we were able to transfer the energy to the others."

"What's the difference between them?"

"You see the three jewels dangling from the bracelet? Those are the three small versions of the jewels we got from Ooray and are what Zack, Kai Li and I have on our necklaces: mine is the blood-red crystal, shaped like a water droplet and called the Timeless Teardrop, the symbol of compassion for the collective history of suffering and hope of humanity throughout the ages; Zack's is the sapphire blue TrueHeart, the heart-shaped protector of self and beacon of love; and Kai Li's is the diamond-like flame held in the base of a torch, the Torch of Truth that reflects the light of all universes since the dawning of time, the symbol of enlightenment."

"What about Morningstar?" Esty asked.

"Her gift was the Web of Life. It's the actual bracelet that holds the jewels. It's made of something like silver or platinum…nothing found here on earth and consists of a web of small stars that actually float in three dimensions, connected to each other simply by forces of energy—like magnets. Ooray said it symbolized the connectedness of all people and things, throughout the history of time."

"I had no idea, Liyah. I guess things moved so fast last time you were here. I was shocked enough at the power of these gifts, let alone all that was happening, I didn't look closely enough. They're astounding! But what about Morningstar's necklace?"

"It's made of the same material as the bracelets, only bigger. And there is no jewel connected to it."

"So that gets us back to the differences, right?" asked Esty, teasing her friend a little.

Liyah chuckled. "Yes, it does. So…the main thing I've found, in playing with my gift and having seen the others use theirs, is this: Each jewel enhances a gift that the wearer already has. For Morningstar it is her understanding of the connectedness of all things; for Zack, strength, and honor; for Kia Li, pursuit of knowledge and truth; and for me, compassion and empathy. You might say they are our superpowers." Liyah laughed again. "Except that the energy of the necklaces is much stronger than that of the bracelets."

Esty studied her own necklace, the split heart she and Ahmad shared. "How do you mean?"

"I guess what I'm seeing is that it's all about sort of infusing your power into the necklace, by believing in yourself and concentrating on what you want to do. In this way, your necklace is as powerful as mine once you find your inner power or powers. For instance, my gift of compassion is enhanced and I can pass its essence on to others. To kind of make them see, or feel, what I do…to teach them."

"So, for Zack that might be bravery or something?"

"Yeah. But at the same time, all of us can use the basic energy within us to help us in certain ways beyond that…like starting a fire, moving an object, or weaving an energy grid around ourselves or others to protect them, keep us safe, or hold others at bay. And we can even get others to look back at their lives or see history in person…to help them see our connectedness, or the truth, or to gain knowledge or empathy at lightning speed."

"And what about time travel?" Esty questioned. "Zack spoke to me about that. How you guys travel back and forth yet little time passes, if any."

"Well, that's still a bit of a mystery to me, actually. I'm still working on it. No time passed when we first met and spent a week in that strange place. When I came home, I was still in the same place as when I sort of *left*…I was in the square looking for my brother. This past spring, time passed as usual, I call it *real time,* but I don't know about the others. I get the feeling that this time we are spending now will be the same. Maybe it only happens when I meet up in faraway places with Morningstar and everyone. I don't really know, yet."

"What makes the bracelet different from the necklace?"

Liyah pointed to the jewels in the bracelet. "These light up if someone needs me. If it is Zack who wants my attention the blue sapphire lights up, same for the others. But if its Morningstar than the band vibrates. I can travel to see them by simply holding the jewel and thinking of the person. Or I can travel anywhere by holding the jewel on my necklace and concentrating on where I want to go. If I need to contact Kai Li, I would simply hold the Torch in my palm and he'll see my Teardrop light up on his band."

Esty stared wide-eyed at Liyah. "It's all crazy, isn't it?"

Liyah nodded. "Yeah. You could definitely say that!"

"I don't have a bracelet, so what can I do with my necklace? I haven't seriously tried much, other than holding it and feeling the energy vibrate through my body." She giggled lightly. "However, I did get insight into what happened at Re'im by concentrating and seeing a kind of vague playback video of it. I also broke a glass one time at the dinner table when I tried to move it toward me. I wasn't even touching it, but it shattered into pieces. My dad was watching out of the corner of his eye and I thought he was gonna have a stroke. He doesn't ask about it, but I think he hasn't gotten over it." A broad smile broke out across her face.

Liyah laughed. "I know what you mean. I feel guilty that I haven't done enough…learning by practicing, that is. But what I do know is that energy can be magnified through both the bracelet and the necklace, like from light, magnetic sources, heat...or even thoughts, and then channeled through your body. It's your mind that controls it. Ooray sort of suggested that once you master some of this you can even do it without either device."

Esty stared blankly at her. "Really?"

"Yeah. I think Ooray gave us these things to kind of make us aware of the powers we already have. Especially the necklaces, which, like I said, bring out the unique powers we already have inside us."

"I don't know what *my* power is," Esty lamented.

"It might be many small things or one or two big things, Esty. And what we all found is that what we learn from each other we add to our own. For instance, Zack can be pretty much a sarcastic pain in the ass sometimes, if you didn't notice….but you should have seen him before."

Liyah winked at Esty, then chuckled. Esty smiled back.

"But he has great strength in him and a lot of love," Liyah continued. "Ooray brought that out through his gift. And our individual powers rubbed off on each other: Morningstar, Zack, Kai Li, and me. It's what kind of gives life to our mission. We can see how it might work—how you can change the world from the bottom up, eventually perhaps even without any *gifts* at all, once it gets going."

"Well, something has to happen, doesn't it?" Esty replied, somber. "I mean look around, life, as usual, isn't working here, is it?"

Liyah fixed her eyes on her friend's. "No. It isn't. And it hasn't worked for a very long time."

There was a rap on the door. They glanced at each other and hurriedly shuffled their jewelry under Liyah's pillow.

"Time to come down and help with dinner prep, girls."

Seventeen

AT 5:30 P.M. Ahmad and a few of the men left at the Dawn were in the largest office on the second floor, disconnecting the sections of the smaller printing press as directed. Everyone else had left for home, including his boss.

He had some experience with the actual printing process since he had worked in the print rooms the previous year before being elevated to an actual journalist—his dream job. The Dawn had completed the printing of the main paper which had already been picked up by the major distributors, who would deliver to outlets throughout Gaza, the West Bank, and even Jerusalem, for redistribution to resale stores, businesses, and individual homes.

The smaller press Liyah's dad had asked him to shelter in the basement occupied half of the office they were in but was maybe a tenth the size of the main press, which took up most of the first floor and poked up into a big part of the second floor...producing a loud non-stop repetitive hum, like the wheels of a locomotive rumbling down the iron sections of track.

This smaller press was Ahmad's favorite. Like its much larger brother, it was a web-fed offset press, used to efficiently print off newspapers, but at a slower pace, so it's hum was more tolerable. He could actually get his journalistic work done in the room, on the rare occasions when he had to help oversee its operation. For both presses, a huge roll fed the paper in a continuous stream into a set of printer cylinders: the plate cylinder, specially made for each job containing the images and typeface to be transferred to the paper; the blanket cylinder, a roller covered by a layer of rubber that transfers the image to the paper; and the pressure cylinder which applies pressure to the paper to create the final inked image.

But what Ahmad liked most about this small press was that it was new, specially modified by a top German printing company to add a sheet-fed paper option. Fully integrated into the sets of rollers, it provided for the printing of brochures, business cards, magazines, small books, advertising pieces, and other business-related applications. These were higher dollar margin applications, and the demand for these had been increasing. If anything happened to the main press, the Dawn could survive on this press alone.

Once Ahmad had disconnected all four sections containing the roller sets used to create the colors, the black and white printer, the roller and sheet feeder sections, and the cutters and bin collectors for outputs, one of the workers approached him.

"What do you want us to do with all this, boss?"

Ahmad grinned at him. "Boss?"

"Yeah," the man laughed. "You might be still wet behind the ears, but the *big man* says you're in charge of whatever we're doing here."

Two others joined the first, all standing in front of him.

"Well, thanks for showing up," Ahmad said, tongue in cheek. "The *big boss,* as you say, wants us to take this press and secure it in the basement. He's afraid if this place ends up as part of a bombing, we could lose everything. But if we shelter this below, it might survive an attack."

"Okay," replied the one to his right, "Just tell us what you need."

Ahmad pointed to the sections he had disconnected. "I placed the protective covers for these on the far side, next to each. I think it will take two of us to move each section. The first room on the right down there should be big enough to store everything."

"What about that roller section and the paper roll?"

"I think if we work together to move the housing we can get it down there, but that paper is super heavy and awkward, so not sure about that. Probably best to leave it. We can always buy paper."

"Sure thing, boss," the third man said, the others chuckling as they moved to begin the process.

Ahmad laughed along with them. "Okay, you can cut that out. Let's get moving. I'd like to get out of here at a reasonable hour tonight. I got a late start on this, but if we move fast, we might be able to do this in a few hours."

Much to Ahmad's chagrin, it took over two hours to move all the pieces of the press into the basement room. He let two of the others leave about 7:00 after several explosions were heard not too far away. He and the last remaining helper added another level of protection by covering the sections of the press with layers of large cardboard boxes, topped off with crisscrossed thick metal strapping to protect from any possible puncture due to the possibility of falling debris should the floor above cave in.

No one was left in the building except the two of them. Ahmad locked the door to the basement room and turned off the lights on the first and second floors. He was about to lock the main entrance door when he remembered he left his jacket on the back of the chair in his office. He motioned to the co-worker.

"Go ahead, Amir. I've got to get something out of my office. See you tomorrow. And thanks for your help."

"See you then, Ahmad. Have a good evening." The young man swung open the big glass door, stepped outside, and disappeared down the dimly lit street.

Ahmad made his way to his office. He took his jacket from the chair and put it on, removing his cell phone from the pocket. Stopping in front of the receptionist's area, he texted Esty.

Sorry E.

Meant to text earlier. Had to do a special project
for Liyah's dad. Got caught up...you know.
Was hoping to get out of here earlier.
Bit late but I'll still try to make it make by 7:30
Liyah's dad is giving me some time off to help
find Hanna.
XOX

Stepping into the glass foyer, he took his keys from his pocket, locked the inner door, then began typing the code into the keypad on the wall to set the alarm. After pressing the last key, the red "Alarm On" message flashed. As he turned to open the door to the street, a high-pitched whining sound caught his attention. He glanced back at the alarm, but this sound was too high for that. It's intensity grew quickly, then the pitch became lower. Ahmad's eyes widened. It took him only an instant to recognize what was happening. His body froze, his mouth opened, and his eyes looked up.

WHAM!

An artillery shell hit the center of the building, blowing Ahmad and the glass door into the middle of the street.

The battery-activated alarm went off, sounding its ear-piercing warning.

Whoop…Whoop…Whoop….Whoop

Eighteen

DINNER GOT STARTED late at the Al Rahim household. It was already past the usual 7:00 start. Liyah's dad sat in his traditional position at the head of the table, looking down the length of it to his wife at the opposite end. Liyah and her brother sat next to each other on the left side, Liyah next to her mom, Khalib next to his father. Across from Khalib was Esty, the chair between her and Mrs. Al Rahim vacant.

"Honors, David?"

"Yes, yes. Of course, dear." He lifted his water glass.

"I apologize for holding up dinner. I had a late meeting in Gaza, and it went on a lot longer than I planned. Then on my way home, I got a call from the mayor of Gaza City. The call lasted an hour...I've actually been sitting in the driveway for half of it." He scanned the faces at the table. "Cheers to everyone!"

Those who were close enough to each other clinked their glasses. Liyah's dad then glanced at the seat next to Esty.

"I see someone is missing. Something happen to Ahmad?"

"I got a text from him just a little while ago, Mr. Rahim," Esty replied. "He said he had been working on something for you. I tried to text him back and then called him, but there was no answer." Esty's eyes betrayed her attempt to not appear concerned. She gathered herself together. "We thought maybe you knew. I tried to tell him to come anyway. But it appears he went home."

"Sorry, Esty. No. I expected he'd already be here."

Liyah's mom glanced at Esty. "I'm sure we'll see him tomorrow."

"For sure," Liyah added, trying to cheer up her friend. "Dinner looks yummy, Mama. Lamb kabobs with stuffed veggies is one of my favorites."

"Well, I'm surprised there's anything left of it…sitting in the oven this long. And I hope you're all not over-stuffed from all the pita bread and hummus you had to eat while we waited." She scowled lightly across the table at her husband.

He nodded in recognition of her disapproval. "Yes, dear. Sorry again."

Khalib picked up a pack of matches lying next to the silver candle holder in front of his dad and handed it to him.

He took the matches from his son, looking a bit confused, before breaking into a smile. "Yes, yes. Thank you, Khalib. I almost forgot." He turned to his right and handed them to Esty. "Khalib and I were talking yesterday and thought it would be nice if you would light the candles for us tonight…like you and your father did the last time we were all together. I'm sorry that your dad couldn't make it."

"Of course." Esty took the matches from him and struck one of them against the narrow sandpaper strip. The flame ignited. Her nose crinkled as it reacted to the smell of the sulfur drifting upward.

She pulled the candle and base closer and moved the flame toward it. Once the wick accepted the flame, she gently blew out the match. Everyone at the table grew silent. Liyah looked across at Esty. It was such a loving thing her friend and father did for her mother and each other. She could feel the moisture gathering in the corners of her eyes.

"In the absence of my father, I light this candle in remembrance of my mother. Of her kindness and caring for us, and for all Israelis and Palestinians alike. In her life she grew to love the Old City of Jerusalem that sheltered and connected Jews, Muslims, and Christians…those who have shared life in the Levant, together, for thousands of years. I hope to follow in her path. It's why I work as a tour guide there."

She stood up, reaching the candlestick down the table, touching the wavering flame to the wick of the other candle.

"I light this second candle, knowing that my mother is now with us here at this table, at this gathering of friends, and with her husband, my father—wherever he may be at this moment. And I wish for peace across our land in this very difficult time, where the anger and ill will of a few is the cause for so much pain to the many."

She sat back in her seat and scanned the somber, loving faces of those around her. Tears trickled slowly down Liyah's cheeks. It seemed that no one was willing to break the magical calm and closeness of such a moment.

After a short pause, Liyah's dad cleared his throat. "That was wonderful, Esty. Thank you. Let's all be thankful for our advantages and the gift of every meal. And mindful of the messages of the candles; hopeful that things will calm down…that this so-called *war* will not actually happen. Now, if you will all pass your dishes up, I'll serve you. And we can begin what I know will be another delicious meal presented through the artistry and diligence of my lovely wife, Rania."

Liyah's mom smiled at her father. "Always the clever one, how you smooth things over, David. But I accept, as always."

Khalib caught the wink his dad passed back to his mom and snickered. He glanced across the table. "So, Esty. What are the plans to find your friend? Seems like you and Liyah are on another kidnap-solving mission."

She accepted her plate from Liyah's dad and set it down in front of her. "I'm waiting to hear from Ahmad. There was a bit of a mix-up tonight but maybe I'll know something tomorrow. And our *mission* as you call it could likely involve you, too, you know."

He laughed. "Just say the word."

"Don't egg him on, Esty. He's tripping over himself enough as it is having you here."

Khalib turned and frowned at his sister.

After everyone completed their dinner, the table was cleared by Liyah and her mother. As they shuffled between the dining room and kitchen to the sound of rattling dishes and chiming silverware, the phone rang. Liyah's dad excused himself and answered the one in the den.

Liyah set the final dessert dish on the table, and her mother took her seat. As her father returned to the dining room her mom looked up at her husband's pale face. "Who was that, dear?"

"It was the hospital. Something's happened to Ahmad."

Nineteen

"WHAT!?" GASPED ESTY. "What do you mean?"

"There was an explosion at the Dawn. No details yet. The police found him in the street. At the hospital, they pulled his work badge from his pocket. He has no family here, so they called me."

Liyah's mother rose to her feet, her voice anxious. "Well, how is he, David?"

"They have him in the emergency room. He's unconscious."

"Oh, my God!" screamed Esty.

"Allah!" echoed Liyah, staring over at her friend.

"Can we go see him?" asked Khalib.

"Not yet. He's apparently sustained other injuries as well, and they're working on him. The hospital rooms are closed to visitors except for rare exceptions, and no will be allowed in the ER. We'd just be waiting there all night anyway. They suggest we go in the morning. They'll call us if there is any change before then."

Esty began to sob. "Oh, Ahmad! My Ahmad!"

"I need to go to the Dawn and see about the damage. I hope no one else was there." He grabbed his keys from the hook next to the hall bureau. "I'll call your mother, Liyah, as soon as I know more. But I suggest you all get your rest while you can."

"How is that possible, Baba?"

"I know it may sound impossible but try. The morning will come before you know it and we'll see how he's doing then."

As the front door clicked shut behind him, his wife turned to the others. "Come. Help me clear the table and do the dishes. We need to stay busy. It will help."

Esty continued to sob as she and Liyah cleaned and dried. Khalib quietly helped his mother put things away. It was close to 9:30 by the time everything was done. Liyah hung her dish towel on the knob of the small door below the sink.

"I think you should all go upstairs and try to get some sleep," said her mom. "I'll read in the den until your father comes home, Liyah."

Esty's crying had lessened but her pallor was deathlike, her eyes vacant. She and Liyah retired to their room, and Khalib to his.

At midnight the door latch clicked again, and Liyah's dad made his way to the den. His wife looked up from her book, her eyes questioning.

"It's not good news. The building is virtually destroyed."

"Oh, David! What happened?"

"The police tell me three buildings were hit along the street."

"Missiles?"

"No. Artillery. Similar effect, but more worrisome. It means they're softening the targets for an invasion. I'm sure of it."

"Allah! What are we going to do?"

"I don't know. The main press is destroyed along with most of the building. Thankfully, Ahmad had secured the smaller press in the basement. It may have survived, but the debris from the blast is six feet deep. I'll go back with a team when the sun comes up."

"What can I do?"

"I'm sure the girls will be up early if they aren't still up. You can bring them to the hospital and get a reading on

Ahmad. We need an adult there to keep things sane and discuss the situation with the doctors and staff."

"They're basically adults now, David. They've been through so much this past year."

"Well, you know what I mean. They may be a little irrational depending on Ahmad's condition. And he's really our responsibility now."

"Yes, of course, dear." She stood up and took hold of his hand. "Come to bed. We'll deal with it in the morning. You look tired."

"That's because I am. Okay, let's head on up."

At 7:00 a.m. he was already back at the Dawn, and the girls were sitting at the table having breakfast.

Liyah's mother put a bowl of oatmeal in front of each of them. "Did you girls sleep at all?"

"I managed to cry myself to sleep," Esty replied. "But Liyah was up all night."

Her mother turned to her. "Why is that sweetie?"

"I don't know. Just thinking I guess."

"Can we go to the hospital soon?" Esty asked.

"Visiting hours are in about an hour. So, yes. After you eat and freshen up."

Liyah held a spoonful of oatmeal in front of her mouth. "Any word?"

"No, dear. Nothing. That could be a good thing, though."

"How do you mean?"

"I mean if there was any really bad news we'd have heard."

Esty stared at Liyah and quickly shoveled down a few mouthfuls. "I'm gonna get ready now. How soon can we leave?"

"When you're ready. Liyah's father left the keys for me and arranged a ride to the Dawn for himself."

"I can drive," Esty replied.

"Nice of you to offer, Esty, but we agreed that with that sticker on your windshield, given the current circumstances, we better not take that car in town."

"I see. Okay. Well, c'mon Liyah. We need to get moving."

"Go ahead, dear. I'll get a note together to leave for Khalib. He probably won't be up until after we get back, but I don't want him to be concerned that we've all been taken somewhere."

"It's awful that anyone has to worry about something like that, Liyah replied. Just another sign of these sad awful times we seem to be living in."

TWENTY

LIYAH, HER MOTHER, and Esty approached the reception area at the hospital. The same hospital Esty had visited before—the Al-Amal International Hospital

The woman behind the counter glanced up over the top of her glasses. "Can I help you?" She looked past Liyah's mom to Esty. "Oh, hello dear. Back again? You created a bit of a stir here the other day. What can I do for you today?"

"Stir?" asked Liyah, glancing at Esty and then the receptionist.

"Ah, sorry," replied the woman. "I must have mistaken you for someone else."

Liyah looked at Esty again, her brow furrowed, questioning.

"Later," mouthed Esty, under the radar of Liyah's mother.

"So, how can I help you?" repeated the receptionist.

Liyah's mother spoke up. "We're looking for a patient. Ahmad Aziz,"

The woman typed into the console, waited a moment, then scanned the screen. "He's in a special section of the ICU. You'll have to check in at the desk…third floor, follow the signs. Just write your names on these tags and stick them to your shirt, but not your jackets or outerwear." She pointed to the elevators.

The three proceeded to the elevators, pushed through the swinging doors that marked the entrance of the ICU, then stopped in front of the nurse's station.

"We're here to see Ahmad Aziz," Mrs. Al Rahim said to the nurse sitting at the station, reviewing a chart.

The nurse looked up. "He's not taking any visitors today."

"Not taking visitors?"

"I mean he's not able to see anyone. He's being evaluated."

"Evaluated?" asked Esty.

"Yes," replied the nurse, studying Esty's blond hair. "Are you family?"

"Ah…yes," replied Liyah. "We're the only family he has. He was an orphan. He works for my dad, and we are close." She pointed to Esty. "And she is his girlfriend."

"I see. Well, come with me."

The nurse escorted them into the main body of the ICU, then separated a few of the wide plastic strips dangling from the ceiling, holding them aside while the others entered the bed area where Ahmad was being treated.

Liyah stared at the bank of monitors to the far side of the bed, beeping and blinking their messages to anyone who might care. Her eyes then shifted to Ahmad. He was lying on his back, his chest tilted slightly upward. His body was covered by a sheet and blanket most of the way up. His arms rested by his side, bandaged in various areas. His head was wrapped in gauze, only his eyes visible. A mouthpiece from a ventilator covered the remainder of his face. Next to him were two IV poles. She took her eyes off him and glanced wide-eyed at Esty, who was already looking at her with tears in her eyes.

"Oh, Allah," whispered Liyah's mom.

A doctor stood at the bedside, fully absorbed, shining a pen-type flashlight into Ahmad's eyes, and moving it side to side.

The nurse spoke up. "Doctor?"

The doctor finished the short test and turned around.

"These people are the patient's family."

He came around the side of the bed and nodded to them.

"How is he?" Liyah asked. The lump she could feel in her throat distorted the words as they came out.

"He's been in a coma."

"Coma?" cried Esty, grasping Liyah's hand like a vice.

"Yes. He lost consciousness during the explosion. I'm assuming you are all aware of what happened?"

"We know there was one, Liyah's mother replied. "But we didn't get any details, other than he was found in the middle of the street."

"He has some wounds from flying glass and scrapes from sliding along the road… on his upper body, arms, and head. Yet amazingly, no broken bones. He's unresponsive to sound, either due to damage to his hearing or shock. We should know more as he comes out of the coma."

"So, he will come out?' asked Esty. "When?"

Liyah could sense the desperation in her friend's voice. A feeling of shame crept into her mind. *All the times I let jealousy creep in my heart. Selfish? Self-centered? I was falling in love, wasn't I? Maybe from a distance…but still.* She squeezed Esty's hand.

"It's not certain. His eyes can follow the light. It's a good sign. The rest of him is pretty broken, but the sooner he comes out the better his chances of avoiding any permanent damage."

Esty squeezed back on Liyah's hand.

"Talk to him, Esty," Liyah coaxed.

Esty looked at her. "He can't hear."

"If he could hear anything, it wouldn't be the noises of this room, or the beeping of the monitors, or the doctor. It would be you."

"But…"

"Go ahead. Get close. Let him know it's you. Wouldn't Ooray say there is magic in our hearts and music that only *it* can communicate?"

As Liyah's mother began a conversation with the doctor, Esty let go of her friend's hand and stepped closer to the side of the bed. She gently took Ahmad's hand in hers, but there was no reaction. No reciprocating squeeze. No movement of his body. No tilt of his head.

Esty shifted her eyes to Liyah, who nodded and whispered. "Tell him who you are."

Slipping her necklace over her head, Esty placed it in his hand and bent her lips down close to his ear. She looked at his lifeless face and began to cry ever so lightly. She wrapped her fingers around his, pressing the pendent tight in his hand, then whispered into his ear.

As she began to draw back, Esty felt Ahmad's hand resist ever so weakly. She studied his face, then burst into tears and knelt next to the bed, placing her head on his chest.

The doctor gently helped her back to her feet. "Sorry, you'll have to be careful of his wounds."

"But he responded!" she protested.

"It may only seem that way. It can happen even with people in deeper states of unconsciousness."

"No. I know he is coming back. He squeezed my hand and I saw life in his eyes."

"I hope so. We'll see. We'll let you know if we see any progress, dear," added the nurse as the two of them pulled her away.

After gathering herself together, she thanked the doctor and asked the nurse where Ahmad's clothes were. The nurse pointed to a narrow set of cupboards that was used to block the individual patient areas from each other. "The one on the far right is his things are."

While Liyah's mother gathered some last details from the doctor, Liyah watched as Esty pulled the cabinet door open and scanned the interior. Leaning in she slid the clothes hangar containing his shirt and pants to the side, seeming to rifle through them before finally extracting something and slipping it into her purse. She then removed a pen, scribbled something on a small piece of paper, and stuck it in the pocket of Ahmad's shirt. After returning the pen to her purse, she closed the cabinet and joined the others.

In the car, on the way home, Liyah comforted her friend, still sobbing now and again, until the sobs gave way to sniffles.

"What did you put in his shirt pocket?"

"A note," replied Esty. "It said I have his cell."

"Why did you take it? Won't he want to use it when he wakes up...so he can call you?"

Esty's throat tightened up. "We don't know when that might happen, do we? And we need his contacts to find Hanna. He actually sent me the contact info of one person in Gaza City, but with Ahmad unable to text him, we'll have to do that now. If any message comes from my phone, I'm sure it will be ignored. It occurred to me we need to set up the meeting from Ahmad's phone. He trusts Ahmad."

"What made you so sure he had a chance to wake up?"

"His hand pressed back against mine, Liyah. And I saw a tear in his eye."

"What did you say to him before that?"

"I said I loved him, and that there was much still to do. That our mission is just beginning…and requires his presence."

Twenty-One

AFTER LUNCH, LIYAH and Esty headed out the door and started down the walkway to the street. Liyah wore a full-length shift, casual shoes, her favorite dark blue hijab, and a light button-down beige sweater. Esty had on her sneakers and jeans, zip-up jacket, and a black hijab that Liyah had insisted on, to cover up her blond hair.

"What a day!" Liyah gushed. "You'd think it was still summer."

Esty sighed as she breathed in the smoky smell of the rows of red poppies with their black centers, still blooming, covering the ground between the walkway and the Jaffa orange hedge that blocked any neighbor's view of Esty's car.

"It's nice, Liyah. It's hard, though, to fully enjoy it under the circumstances."

"I know," Liyah replied. "But let's make the best of..."

"Where are you girls sneaking away to?" Liyah's mother shouted from the stoop at the front door. "Were you going to tell me at all?"

"Sorry, Mama. We're headed into Gaza city to meet with a friend...taking a taxi...only be a few hours or so."

"Well, be careful," her mom huffed. "It's not safe anymore. Your father would not approve."

"I know. We'll be okay. We both have phones and we'll call if we need anything."

"See that you do, please." She turned, making her way back inside.

They passed through the swinging gate to the street just as the taxi arrived and slid into the back seat. Liyah looked at the driver in the rearview mirror. "Café Saker, please."

The street was busy this time of day, but less than twenty minutes expired before the sign with the falcon appeared above the café and the car pulled to a stop.

Liyah read the meter and handed the man the fare plus tip.

"*Shukran*," she said as thy exited the car.

The cabby nodded and drove off.

"Likely not many women in here, Esty. I'll do most of the talking."

Esty chuckled. "That's good, Liyah. Because I speak only very basic conversational Arabic anyway. But maybe you can keep the conversation in English for my benefit."

"Okay. I would have liked to have Khalib along," Liyah replied. "A male presence, you know. But I don't know how this guy would react to more people knowing about him. The two of us is bad enough…plus us being women. And he's expecting only Ahmad." She pushed open the door and they entered the darkness of the dimly lit café. "It's going to be interesting."

"He said he'd be at the same table in the back," Esty replied, "whatever that means."

They made their way past the order counter, past a line of tables along the wall by the window to the street, where people were busy typing away on their computers or chatting on their cell phones.

Liyah didn't get out to café's much. It was still mostly a male thing to do, she mused. The café seemed a bit quiet to her. Maybe because the morning crowd was gone, or people were feeling generally uneasy any place outside their homes…even though she didn't think the homes were safe any longer, either.

The room opened up to a larger area of about twenty-five tables, about half occupied. In the back, along the rear wall, were five tables. Two were occupied by a single individual. At one end a man was sitting sipping a coffee, making notes on a pad. On the other end, three tables separating him from the first was another man staring at his cell phone. Liyah looked at Esty. "What do ya think?"

"I'd go with the one with the pad."

"Okay," agreed Liyah. "Let's see."

As they approached his table, he looked up.

"Malik?" asked Liyah.

"No. Can I help you?"

"Oh. Sorry to bother you."

They stepped away, glancing over at the other table at the opposite end. "Must be him," said Esty. "He's still occupied with his phone. Looks like he didn't hear us say his name."

"Damn, we'll hope so," Liyah replied. "Well, take in a breath. Let's go over."

They approached the older man sporting a full black beard, wearing a green cap, and sitting at the corner table. It took a moment before he noticed them. He set his phone down and stared at them, saying nothing.

"Malik?" asked Liyah.

"Yes," the man answered, looking puzzled.

Liyah bowed slightly. "*As-salaam alaikum.*"

"*Wa-alaikum salaam,*" he replied, tilting his head like a quizzical bird.

"I'm Liyah, perhaps Ahmad has spoken of Esty, here…his girlfriend?"

An expression of concern flooded across Malik's face. He glanced at Esty and then back at her. "Yes, he did. However, I don't recall that he mentioned a name during our recent conversation. But–"

"I know this may be awkward, and we apologize for this surprise. Ahmad must have had a premonition because he sent your contact to Esty, telling her not to use it unless it was in an absolute emergency. She shared it with me only because she isn't fluent in Arabic. I'd like to keep this conversation to English if you don't mind…so she can be part of it."

He looked over at Esty again.

"So what emergency? Where is Ahmad?"

"In the hospital. Artillery fire hit the Filastin Dawn. You probably heard. He was the only one there. The exploding shell blew him into the street. He's in a coma."

Malik raised his eyebrows. "Sit. Sit. Can I get you something?"

Liyah pulled up two chairs and joined him. "No thank you," Liyah replied. "We have to be back soon, and we would like to maximize our time with you."

"Is Ahmad going to be all right?"

"We don't know yet. We are hopeful."

"May Allah be with him. I will pray for him."

"Thank you," replied Esty. "Ahmad said he had sent you a picture of my friend Hanna."

"Yes."

"Can you tell us anything?"

"I do have some information, but I don't see how that's going to do you any good."

"Why not?" asked Liyah.

"Because I cannot expose myself by searching directly for your friend Hanna. Ahmad was going to do that. It would be too dangerous for me. I don't want them hunting me down. I'm an easy target."

"We're going to do that now," Liyah replied.

"And who exactly are *you?* Malik questioned, his tone a bit acidic. "That isn't clear to me yet."

"I'm a friend of both Ahmad and Esty. My dad runs the Dawn."

Malik softened. "I see. Your father is well known…to both sides of this conflict. He treads a fine line. But I respect him. Many of the hardcore extremists both in Hamas and the Israeli government have threatened him. I believe some of these tried to kill him some time ago. He is a brave man."

"You are Hamas, aren't you?" asked Esty.

"Yes, but I am, what you might call, *retired.*"

He turned to Liyah. "But neither do I accept in any way the brutal treatment by Israelis of our fellow

Palestinians…for generations. How exactly do you think, as women…or should I say girls, you are expecting to do what Ahmad was asking for help with? This would be a challenge even for him and what few people he could enlist. To take on such a perilous task."

"We might surprise you," replied Esty. "What we need is mostly a lead from which to start. A place to begin."

He studied her, his eyes scanning her face, black hijab, and the blond braid sneaking out from under it.

"You'll not go far with that pale skin and blond hair. You'd best be covering up better than you are…you're a dead giveaway. And I do mean dead."

Esty stared back at him, her eyes betraying a sudden sense of fear.

Liyah placed her hand on his wrist and locked her eyes on his. She concentrated her thoughts, sending a wave of energy through her fingers.

He jerked his arm away, staring wide-eyed at her hand, before bringing his attention back to her.

"What was that?"

"Just something to give you some assurance that we will be okay. What can you tell us?"

Malik scratched his beard, his eyes shifting back and forth between the two of them. After a short pause, he spoke.

"These tunnels in Gaza go for hundreds of miles. They are literally an underground escape and supply system. The entrances are well hidden. Many of the tunnels are wide enough to transport vehicles and equipment. They are shaped like cylinders and tiled…kind of like a mini version of the London Tube underground, with self-contained electrical and air systems. Many others are much smaller, barely accommodating an adult man. And still, others of rock and dirt, and even more narrow, forcing people to bend over or at times even crawl. Without a map, it's impossible to know your way around. Unless you memorize the major sections and know how to read the coded markings at the intersections."

He pulled a piece of paper out of his shirt pocket. "There is a tunnel under the Al-Amal Hospital, north of here…not too far. There is a person working as a maintenance man there. He fixes the generators in the basement. His codename is Hawk. He has a black curly mustache and no beard. He said he thinks your friend might be being kept in one of the main tunnels in the center or possibly farther south of the city, near a large mosque. Both of those places are hard to find and well-guarded. The best way in is to already be in the tunnel system. He can get you in where one of the main tunnels begins…there at the Al-Amal.

"What would he be expecting from us?" asked Liyah.

"Nothing. But he would have been expecting Ahmad. I can tell him it will be you. He trusts me implicitly."

"And maybe a few young men," added Liyah.

Malik blinked several times at her, then sighed heavily "You're making it difficult."

"It sounds like a long journey in those tunnels, and we will need some protective assistance just in case."

"Okay. But understand…once you're in I can't be of any further help. You're on your own."

Liyah nodded. "Understood."

"Understood," echoed Esty.

"You will need proof." He handed Liyah the small piece of paper he had been holding in his hand and unfolded it. "This is my stamped *mark*. No other words can be written down on anything. It will be recognized by Hawk. Don't forget his name." He stood up and bowed.

"*Ma'asalaama.* Go with Allah."

"Thank you, Malik," replied Liyah, tilting her head slightly down.

"*Salaam,*" replied Esty.

Twenty-Two

ESTY CLICKED OFF her cell phone and made her way down the stairs and into the living room. Liyah and her father were sitting across from each other, talking, her on the sofa and him in his favorite high-backed leather armchair. She took a seat next to Liyah and set her phone on the coffee table. The sun was already sinking below the window shade, flowing through the panes of glass, penetrating her denim shirt, and instantly warming her. Liyah ended her conversation and turned to her.

"My dad says Ahmad isn't awake yet."

"Well, not exactly Liyah. Don't frighten her. What I said, Esty, was that he has not gained full consciousness, but the nurses have noticed what you mentioned to Liyah…that there's now a reaction to sound and touch and recognition of objects. He's got a ways to go, but they feel this is significant progress. Very encouraging."

Esty let the breath out she had been holding since Liyah spoke. She elbowed Liyah playfully so her father could see as well. "Thanks for the clarification, Mr. Al-Rahim. Did you ever notice how Liyah leaves things out from time to time?"

He laughed. "You two know each other well. You're like sisters, aren't you? Even though it's been less than a year."

Esty nodded. "We've gone through more during that time than most sisters might face in a lifetime. Liyah has been through even more with Morningstar." She smiled. "And of course Zack and Kai Li, which I guess would make them like brothers."

"And don't forget Ahmad," added Liyah.

"Not exactly a *brother*," her dad joked.

Esty scolded them with her finger. "Very funny."

David updated them on the disaster at the Dawn, covering the details of the total destruction of the building, the other buildings destroyed by similar rounds of artillery, and even a missile, and how the small press might be salvaged in its entirety. Esty watched Liyah's eyes remain steady on his, always so full of love for him. Her thoughts began to drift. She considered her relationship with her own father. *It's similar,* she thought. *Both of us are what our parents might consider "responsible" children, even if they didn't know some of the details of our recent adventures.* She smiled to herself. *And we are both following the lead of our dads, loving them with every beat of our hearts, planning to do battle with the outside world, remaining steady…for them, taking care of them, honoring them.*

Not that our moms weren't equally important, she told herself. *No. Not at all. Mother is still very present in my life, even though she's not among the living. Liyah loves hers as well. Maybe it's just that Liyah's mom is more old school. Or maybe it's the nature of the dance between mothers and daughters. Some natural baggage there perhaps. The connections and expectations of mothers throughout human history, the maternal bond butting up against the coming of age of their daughters; same-sex instinctual understandings facing the tug of war between freedom and suffocation. Wasn't my own relationship with my mother like this, after all? I guess maybe when she died all that was forgiven, and imminently forgotten. And all that was left was simply love without the overblown entanglements.*

Why not so with the fathers, she wondered. *Not that there aren't disagreements…big ones at times. But for me and Liyah they appeared not to worry either them or their dads. There was no expectation from them. Not in the same sense at least. They were the traditional fathers, the bread winner warriors, the pillars of strength and hope…holding few judgments, almost no anger, placing little weight on their female shoulders. Maybe that was all reserved for the sons? Same sex again. I…*

"Esty. Esty!" Liyah's voice rang in her ears. "Where did you go?"

"Oh. Sorry." Her face flushed. "Just thinking."

"I guess so. My dad was saying that when Ahmad gets well, he's going to put him in charge of the small press, to keep the paper alive until the Dawn can be rebuilt. It will take time, but it can be done."

"Yes, that's wonderful," Esty agreed. "I hope Ahmad will be up for it."

"He'll be okay, Esty." Liyah placed her hand on Esty's knee. "I just know it."

Liyah's mother's voice drifted in from the kitchen. "You people ready for a snack before dinner? I've trapped Khalib in here helping me. We can bring it to you there or we can sit around the table in the dining room."

"Bring it in here, Rania. Please. Join us. We miss your company."

"Aren't you the smooth one, my husband?"

He laughed so she could hear. "Haven't I always been?"

A few minutes later, Khalib set a tray on the coffee table, holding plates of sliced carrots, broccoli, cauliflower, cherry tomatoes, figs, and pita bread, with two small bowls of hummus and a dill-flavored goat cheese dip. Liyah's mom followed, setting down two pitchers of water, and orange juice along with four small glasses.

They sat together, chatting about the concerns of the day: of Ahmad, the Dawn, the uptick in missile and artillery attacks near the refugee camp and into Gaza City itself, and of the invasion force that Israel was building near the border only a few miles north of Beit Lahia—their home.

As the time got short before the main meal was to be served, the parents began returning the plates and glasses to the kitchen and hand-washing the dishes, leaving the children together in the living room.

Esty's phone rang. It was her father. She excused herself and took the call upstairs in her bedroom.

Liyah turned to her brother. "We need your help, Khalib."

"We?"

"Me and Esty. Ahmad gave Esty the name of a contact in the city, someone who might be able to help us find Hanna."

"Really? Is that a good idea?"

"What do you mean?"

"I mean how are you two going to locate her under these circumstances and get her out…and back across the border into Israel?"

"That's why we need your help, Khalib….Allah. Really. Sometimes I think you're dense."

"Go easy, Sis. I told you I'd help, but things have really heated up, wouldn't you agree? And I don't think mom and dad are going to buy into this."

"They don't have to. Esty and I talked about it as we agreed it would only be a day. We're planning to go to Gaza early in the morning and come home before dinner. It would give us a full day."

Khalib balked.

"C'mon. We have to try *something*! We'll worry about the border thing after we find her."

"*If* you find her. It really is a dangerous thing you're doing. You know that, don't you."

"Of course, but we do have some extra things going for us." She rattled her bracelet.

Khalib stared at her. "Mmm. Yes. I hadn't thought about that lately…must have pushed it out of my mind along with the last trauma we went through." He winked at her. "All right."

"So can you get a couple of your friends to come along?"

"What? Are you crazy?"

"No. A little more help could make the difference. They wouldn't notice as much if there was a small group of us, with you *guys*. Esty and I stand out a bit."

"Speaking of that. Maybe Esty should stay here. She's gonna stick out like a sore thumb."

"She's working on that?"

"Working on what? Is she planning to learn Arabic and turn herself into a Muslim with black hair and darker skin?"

Liyah shrugged. "I don't know, Khalib. Just go with this, would you?"

Khalib studied her. "Well…I'll see what I can do. I suppose it's not much more dangerous than sitting here waiting for the next missile to land on top of us."

Liyah hugged him, squeezing him tight. "Thanks!"

"Yeah, yeah." He began prying her off of him. "Now let go of me."

Esty entered the living room as Khalib finally extracted himself from his sister.

"It was my dad. He wants me home. Everyone knows there's going to be a full invasion soon. The IDF is pretty out front about it, apparently. And it's likely to happen anytime now. We already know they've been ramping up the missile and artillery attacks. The Prime Minister is referring to it as *softening the beaches*."

"What did you tell him?"

"I asked for one more day. He didn't like it but agreed. He said he'd let the border know that his car would be coming through, and to be on the lookout for it…with some passengers. In case your family wants to get out, too. At least until it all blows over."

"Doesn't look like it's going to blow over this time," replied Khalib.

"Stop it, Khalib," insisted Liyah. "You're not helping."

Suddenly a loud explosion rocked the house. The air in the room compressed, pushing violently against their eardrums. The windows on their side of the living room and kitchen bowed in like drumskins made of plastic. Small pebbles, dirt, and other debris pelted the side of the house. Several panes shattered, sending shards of glass a few feet from where they were standing.

Liyah's mother screamed from the kitchen.

Twenty-Three

PUFFY CLOUD FACES and shifting forms drifted slowly across the bright blue sky, making their way toward an unknown destination—like sea turtles floating through a never-ending ocean. She felt her hair caress her forehead, disturbed ever so gently by a cool west wind. The sun moved between the clouds, peeking in and out, warming her face. Her mind floated along with it, carefree, content.

After a while the sun exited from behind the last of the clouds, it's brilliance returning, growing brighter, and brighter. Then suddenly it left its place in the sky and rocketed toward her, like a meteor. Unstoppable.

Hanna's eyes flew open.

"Wake up!" a voice shouted. "Time to move on."

Hanna turned her head away from the piercing brightness of the flashlight the guard held pointed toward her face. She tried to come to grips with where she was, what was happening.

"Huh?"

"We have to get out of here. Headed back in the other direction."

"Why?" Hanna asked, still bewildered but more awake.

"It's none of your business, but the Israelis have stepped up the shelling of Gaza City. We have to move south."

"But we just came from there a few days ago, didn't we? I remember being taken through the border fence near my home. You said we were getting away, headed to the city…Gaza."

"I told you too much already."

Hanna pushed against the rock wall, raising herself to her feet while keeping her eyes on him as he moved down the row of fellow captives, kicking each in the side or leg, ordering each to get up.

She glanced at the young man standing next to her in a dirt-streaked white shirt, sleeves rolled up. He wore black khaki pants and had a five-day's worth of beard growth. He had already been standing when she was awakened. She whispered in his ear. "Do you know what's going on?"

"I overheard him talking to that young kid in a black balaclava and skull cap earlier. You know, the one he pals around with. I've been up for a while and was hanging out where the entrance to this room meets the main tunnel."

"It's hard to tell day from night here," Hanna replied. "Isn't it?"

"It seems something very bad is happening in Gaza," the young man continued. "They said we were about to get to some hospital where they planned to release at least a few of us…maybe only the women. Like they did the other day. But all bets are off. Sometimes I think the Israeli government in Jerusalem is more interested in killing every last Hamas person than in rescuing you Jews."

"Us Jews? I assumed you were one of us. You told me your name was Daniel, right? And that you were doing your degree in *astro* something at the university."

"Archaeology."

"Oh, yes. That was it."

"Daniel," the young man continued. "Campbell—Dan Campbell. Many people like me are here from America."

"Do you have family here?"

"No."

"How'd you get in this mess?"

"I was working on a small dig not too far from Re'im, where you got trapped at the Peace and Love concert. You never asked me."

"You could have told me. All this time I was thinking you were from here."

"What difference does it make? We're all stuck here now."

"But why didn't they let you go? They aren't after Americans."

He laughed. "They were looking for people they could brutally kill, to instill fear, and hostages they could trade as barter…to keep the IDF from invading. Or to exchange to keep their Hamas leaders safe. An American would do just fine. No one else really counts, do they? I mean it might as well be just the leaders of both countries in a boxing ring. That would be the best way to handle it, I'd say. We're fodder."

"But at least they'd keep you alive."

"Doesn't really matter. I actually thought that might help. But I didn't have my passport on me. It was a two-day gig, and I wasn't exactly expecting to be captured by terrorists."

"You should tell them," she insisted.

"They won't believe me. And now that we've been through several different tunnels with multiple sets of guards, they don't have any idea how I ended up here. I can't prove anything…And no one is missing me. My family is not expecting to hear from me at all. Last they knew I had left for a few weeks to go to Egypt to take a few days to see the pyramids and then work on another dig with a group of archaeologists from the University in Cairo. No one has any reason to suspect I might be caught up in this, well…bullshit."

Hanna stared at the single dimly lit bulb, positioned above the exit to the room she and all the others were captive in, where that room met the main tunnel. It was the only source of light for the twenty-by-twenty square foot enclosure. The room itself was cruder than the main tunnel, basically a dirt-packed floor with rock walls and ceiling. It appeared to be used primarily for storing supplies and weapons. She had seen a number of these along her journey through the myriad of tunnels over the past few days. The storage bins in this one took the majority of space, leaving little left for the seven of them, packed in like sardines: three other younger men, two older, her, and Daniel.

Esty breathed in the foul dank air around her, crinkling her nose and shaking her head. She then dragged a finger along the wall, moister than the other side rooms they had rested in at times, or spent the night in. *Maybe this wetness combined with the odor of the bodies made it so much worse than before,* she thought. She turned to Daniel.

"This place smells horrible."

"Not nearly as bad as the small alcoves where we have to go to the bathroom."

"Ew! Don't remind me of that."

"You're the one who brought up smells."

"It's all so disgusting," said Hanna. "Humiliating. And what's worse is you have to ask permission to go…then a guard escorts you while you do your business. Might be okay for you but not me. And it's worse than using a Port-O-Potty. I don't think I'll ever get that smell out of my nose."

"Unless they kill us."

Her face dropped. "Stop it…That's scares me."

"Sorry. I don't like it any more than you. But we have to face the reality that we may never get out of here. We've actually been lucky so far."

As Hanna considered his words, her mind brought her back to Re'im. The sudden clatter of gunfire, the screams, explosions, people dropping dead next to her. She glanced at her once-white sneakers, now splashed red by streaks of blood and lightly covered with dust, the dim light bright enough to highlight them clearly, along with her torn jeans and filthy blouse.

"I'm a mess," she lamented.

He studied her dirt-smudged face and the clumps of dark hair sticking to her forehead, the rest of her head covered by a light purple head scarf. His expression became more serious, his voice almost stern.

"You're alive," he replied.

"*Askat!* Shut up!" yelled the guard from the entrance of the tunnel, pointing his automatic rifle at the two of them. "Get over here! We're moving out!"

Twenty-Four

LIYAH RUSHED INTO the kitchen, Esty and Khalib on her heels. Her mother was kneeling on the floor trying to revive her husband who lay on his side, blood dripping down over his cheek.

"What is it?" she shrieked.

Her mother looked up. "He was bending down to take a tray from the oven when the blast hit. He lost his balance and smashed his head against one of the knobs."

Liyah's dad began to come to, struggling to move his limbs and groggily gather his wits.

His wife held him steady. "Stay still, dear. It's okay. I have you."

Liyah instinctively wet a washcloth under cool water from the faucet and held it against the side of her father's head, pressing gently to stem the bleeding.

"Ugh," groaned her dad. "What happened?"

"A missile or something hit close by, dear. You banged your head on the stove. Are you okay…you were out for a minute?"

"I think so." He sat up then tried to stand.

"Easy, Baba," said Liyah, as she and her mother helped him to his feet.

Her mother took the towel from Liyah, turned it inside out, dabbed around his wound, then pressed it down again. She turned to Liyah. "It needs to be looked at. Call Amina, would you? She's a nurse and would know what to do. I'll start walking him over."

Liyah picked up the receiver in the hall to make the call, noting that the rolling blackout the Israelis had implemented on the power lines was not in force at that moment, so she, fortunately, had a dial tone. Rania led her husband out the door and to Amina's, three doors down the walk.

Esty remained in the kitchen with Khalib.

"How long would it take you to get a couple of friends together to help find Hanna?"

He shrugged. "I don't know, a day or so?"

"We need them tonight."

"What?" replied Khalib, incredulous.

"We have to go now."

"Go now? Where?"

"To the hospital."

"You're not making any sense, Esty."

Esty took him by the shoulders. "Look. I have only a day or so to find Hanna. And do you think anyone is going to let us out alone after this? We have to go now. Can you get two guys to meet us at the hospital in an hour…before it gets too dark?"

"Uh…uh," stammered Khalib. "I'll see what I can do."

Liyah entered the kitchen and caught her brother's eye. "About what?

"Ah…"

"We have to try to find Hanna now, Liyah. It's our only opportunity. Your mom and dad will be tied up for a while, and there's still a little daylight left. We could walk to the hospital in an hour…it's only a couple of miles from here, isn't it?"

"Yes, but.."

"But nothing," replied Esty. "We're wasting valuable time."

"We'd have to pack up some stuff."

"Pack what? We'll be back in a day. You and I can bring a backpack with a change and some water. We have to give it a shot…*NOW!*'

Liyah stared blankly at her friend, then looked over at her brother. He smiled nervously. "You've got crazy friends, Sis. But I'm all in. We can't sit here and wait to be bombed into oblivion. Let's at least do something. I'm gonna call two friends and have them meet us at the hospital. I'll tell them what I can to get their interest, without all the details that might scare them. Why the hospital?"

She glanced over at Esty, then back to her brother. "Because that's where the entrance to the main tunnels is."

Khalib took a step back. "Seriously?"

"Yes," replied Esty. "Seriously."

Liyah breathed in deeply, letting her breath out slowly. "Okay then. Khalib, get your school pack and whatever you need. You can call your friends on the way there. Esty and I each have backpacks we can use and can carry extra water. We can pick up some bottles at the hospital. I'll get some snacks from the fridge and leave a note saying not to worry, that something came up we had to take care of and not to worry."

"Good idea," replied Khalib. "Although I'm sure they'll never believe it. What parent would?"

They heard him laugh as he climbed the stairs to his room. Ten minutes later Liyah opened the front door and herded the other two out.

The three stood on the front steps of the Al-Amal hospital less than an hour later, waiting for Kahlib's friends.

"Are you sure they're coming, Khalib?" asked Esty.

"Pretty sure. You never know with these two."

"Well, that's an understatement," Liyah joked nervously.

"People here are more pissed now than they were when I was kidnapped by the terrorists last spring," he replied. "But this time they are more pissed at Hamas as well. And there's nothing to do during the day. They've closed the school. Kids my age want to do something, anything. They have a lot of energy, and they hear the Israeli Army is massing only a few miles from Beit Lahia, ready to storm in. Rescuing an Israeli girl from Hamas is even more intriguing than causing trouble for the Israeli Army."

"But I suspect much more dangerous," replied Esty.

"It's all relative. I think I'd take my chances with a small number of Hamas terrorists over facing down a tank with a stone in my hand, knowing that this time they wouldn't waste a second running me over."

"Khalib!" One of his friends called out from across the street, waving his arm. Both boys crossed the street together and joined him. They were both wearing camo pants and hooded sweatshirts, one red, one black.

Khalib gave each of them a high five. "*Salaam.*"

"You guys coordinate outfits?" Khalib laughed.

"After you called me about the gig, I called Ali," explained the boy in the black sweatshirt. We know some of the Hamas people but don't know who we'll meet, so we figured it best to dress like them…blend in. You know?"

"Good idea. I was worried you might not show."

"No way, man. Wouldn't miss it. Our parents are used to us not being home every night. There's so much chaos now. People have been losing control of everything, and now with more attacks, the chaos has gone viral."

The boy in the red sweatshirt took something black out of the pocket of his pants and handed it to Khalib. "It's a balaclava. We each have one. Never know when you'll need the disguise. Many of these guys wear them."

Liyah jumped in. "We need to get moving, Khalib."

"Yeah, okay." He looked at his friends. "I think you've both met my sister, Liyah. This is her friend, Esty. It's Esty's friend that we need to locate if we can. Limited time though, max forty-eight hours is the guess, if that. Esty has to leave. And if we can get back before then, we also have to survive our parents."

"*Salaam,*" said the boy in the black sweatshirt, nodding to Esty. "I'm Jawad. You already heard his name…Ali."

"*Salaam,*" echoed Ali.

"Let's go," prodded Esty, lifting her backpack from the step where she had rested it while waiting for the boys to show up. She led the others through the massive glass doors and into the lobby of the same hospital she had already become all too familiar to her.

She brought them to the main bank of elevators, then across the hall to the service elevator she had noticed on her last trip there. Once the doors closed Esty pressed the button for Level B, to the basement.

"This is where we have to meet Hawk. Why don't you guys get some more water from the vending machine over there, while I run an errand upstairs? I forgot something. I'll be right back."

As the four of them stepped out of the elevator, Esty pressed the button to the third floor. When the doors opened she headed to the ICU, stopping at the ladies' room just before the entrance. Five minutes later she opened the door and walked past the nurse's station.

"Excuse me," the attending nurse called to her. "Can I help you?"

Esty turned around. She was wearing a black leather overcoat with the collar up, black and white traditional keffiyeh covered her head and wound around her face.

"Nura!" gasped the nurse.

She turned around. "I'm here to see Ahmad Aziz. I know where he is."

The nurse stood with her jaw unhinged. Nura bowed, turned, and headed through the ICU to the area marked by the hanging plastic strips. She paused to still her mind, then slipped through the plastic.

Ahmad lay on his side, sleeping, facing the wall with his back to her.

She moved around the bed, then knelt in front of him. She ran her hand along the side of his face. She felt his warm breath against her palm and began to quietly cry.

Ahmad blinked his eyes open at the sound of her sniffles. He studied the person in front of him, caught for a moment in unknowing. Her eyes met his.

"Esty?" he whispered.

Twenty-Five

LIYAH'S DAD SAT pensively in the comfortable high-backed chair in the small den of his home in Beit Lahia. In his hand, he held the note left by his daughter. He stared down at it over his reading glasses, tapping the fingers of his other hand against the soft arm of the chair, as if performing a piano exercise. His wife entered the room.

"Are you all right, David?"

His fingers stopped tapping. He raised his hand, pressing gently against the white patch on the side of his forehead, and looked over at her. "I'll be fine. Just a few stitches."

"Amina was nice to help us out and stitch you up, but she said you should get checked at the hospital to make sure you don't have a concussion."

He grunted. "How would that look, Rania? They're now filling the ER, rooms, and corridors with men, women, and children with severe cuts and burns, some already dead but the doctors too busy to confirm it."

"Well, don't jump on me. I'm trying to take care of you. You come first."

He softened. "I'm sorry, dear. And I appreciate that. It's just that the Gaza City area, especially the refugee camp near us, has come under almost full attack. People are fleeing their homes by the tens of thousands. It's like a flood. And it won't be long before the hospitals will be completely overrun."

"Yes, I know. Well, as long as you think you're okay." Her eyes focused on the piece of paper in his hand. "She didn't leave any details. What do you think she's up to?"

"It's not only her. It looks like she's dragged the other two in with her. Or maybe it was Esty who dragged her and Khalib in."

"Esty?" his wife questioned.

"Yes. She's looking for her friend, Hanna, remember? Liyah mentioned to me that Esty spoke with her father. Adam's been anxious for her to get home, but Esty's been dragging her feet."

"How would she ever find Hanna?"

Her husband turned his head toward the fractured window, falling silent for a brief moment. "They know if Hanna's alive she's most likely in the tunnels," he said quietly. "I don't think there's any question about that." He turned back. "That's the thing that frightens me. If we don't see them later tonight then I think we have a major problem."

"Allah, what can we do?"

"I have no idea at the moment. But I need to let Adam know what's going on. I'll call him now, then see if I can reach the girls. It's getting late."

As his wife left the room, he picked up the receiver from the phone on the side table. The phone at the other end rang three times before being answered.

"Hello."

"Hello, Adam. It's David Al-Rahim."

"Ah, David. Nice to hear from you. I understand you're holding my daughter captive there." He laughed. "What can I do for you?"

"Actually, it *is* Esty I'm calling about. I wanted to make sure we're on the same page. I know you spoke to her about staying another day."

"Yes. Is that a problem? I'm getting worried, but she seems to be on some sort of mission. I hope she's not bothering you and your family."

"No, no. That's not it at all," he assured Esty's father. "That would never be the case. She's always welcome here. We're so happy to have her."

"So…"

"The thing is, the mission she's on is trying to locate her friend, Hanna."

"I sort of assumed that," Esty's dad replied. "Although she assured me she'd get home quickly…maybe one more day. She knows how concerned I am about the situation there in Gaza. It's not safe for anyone."

"Well, I didn't want to keep any information from you, but it sounds like you're aware of her activity. Liyah's of course glued to her as well on this."

Esty's dad laughed again. "Wouldn't have assumed otherwise. Is Esty available to speak? I'll see that she gets out of your hair and back into mine."

Liyah's dad coughed lightly, clearing his throat. "Well, that's the other part. Esty, Liyah, and— I'm assuming Khalib—seem to be at it again. They went out after dinner, and I haven't heard from them. I got a short, handwritten note saying not to worry, they'd be back soon. But it's getting late and the shelling is increasing by the hour, especially here in northern Gaza. I thought you should know this. We were planning to get her on her way tomorrow."

"I see," replied Esty's dad, pausing as if in thought. "I'm sure they'll be okay, but I'm also well aware of what you're talking about. I was expecting this ramp-up in military activity. I think I mentioned it to you the other day. It's why I'm concerned as well."

"Yes," Liyah's dad replied. "I know, Adam. But I was holding out hope. I guess I never expected it was really going to happen. And certainly not this fast."

"Prospects are dim, David. I get briefed regularly but not on all the top-secret military plans. That's why I told Esty to come home. And bring you folks with her, if you felt the need to get out." He took a breath. "That's how serious I think it's getting. And I'm feeling powerless to do anything about it except provide you with a means, using the cover of my car and the seal of the Prime Minister, to flee to safety. You and your family are welcome to stay with us for as long as you like. I told Esty to tell you."

"She probably told Liyah, but I haven't seen a lot of either of them. Thanks for the offer. I'll see how things go here. The Dawn was blown to pieces in the last artillery barrage, and Ahmad is in the hospital from it. These attacks are getting more frequent."

"Seriously, David? I had no idea about the Dawn. I'm so sorry. I know of some of the sites that have been hit, like the refugee camp and many of the suspected terrorist hide-out spots in Gaza City…but not the Dawn."

"Ahmad was the only one injured in the blast. He was working late…there are some hopeful signs he'll be fine, though. We're trying to salvage the small press, but it will take a while to clear the debris and set up the printing again if it can be done at all."

"It's all so very tragic, isn't it," Esty's dad replied. "About a half a year ago, I thought we had made a real positive movement in the relations here. Our daughters and their friends literally saved Jerusalem from a devastating attack that could have brought major countries into the fray. But now here we are again. This disaster seems to be more focused specifically between Israel and Hamas, but we know the arms and support come from a lot of countries and could have the same *heating up* effect."

"I have to say this is much worse than I've ever seen it here, Adam."

There was a long silence.

"I expect the girls will be back shortly," said David, continuing. "I'll get in touch with them and let you know the plans to get Esty back on the road home."

"Okay, David. I want to talk to you more about the plans I'm working on here that involve you. About creating a joint media program right here in Jerusalem that could make a big difference in the future of the region. It's extremely important and why I need you here for a short bit. I'll try to…"

Liyah's dad tapped his finger against the receiver, then brought it back to his ear.

"Adam?...Adam?"

Twenty-Six

THE DOORS TO the service elevator opened at the basement level. Liyah and the boys were sitting cross-legged on the hall floor next to the bank of vending machines, backs resting against the tiled wall. The boys gasped simultaneously.

"Nura!"

She made her way across the hall, stopping in front of them and Liyah.

"I knew it," mouthed Liyah.

Nura held her hand up briefly to her and winked, trying to avoid the revelation to the others. But it was too late.

"Are you…" Khalib began before he was cut off.

"Nura," Ali said again. "You're Nura."

She nodded. "That's right."

"But…" Khalib stammered again, unable to finish his sentence.

"But what?" asked Jawad. "Of course that's Nura."

"I, uh…"

She unwrapped the keffiyeh and secured it around her neck. Her blond hair fell over her shoulders.

"Esty?" said Khalib, baffled.

"Yes. It's me."

"Oh, Allah," Ali replied, laughing. "You looked just like Nura."

"That's because I am."

Jawad stared at her, his face written with bewilderment. "What?"

"I'm both," said Esty. "But it goes no further than here. No one can know. It's the only way I will survive this mission to save Hanna, and your lives may depend on it as well…Understood?"

She was met with total silence.

"Understood?" she repeated, forcefully.

The boys stood up, their voices forming a chorus. "Yeah, yeah. Understood."

Liyah smiled. "I knew it," she repeated, this time out loud.

Esty smiled back. "I couldn't hold it from you much longer anyway, Liyah. She turned to the others. "But it's essential that I remain disguised, and that if we get out…sorry…when we get out, no one else finds out either. It's too important to what we are doing here in Gaza and Israel. We are trying to restore peace in the Levant. To bring back the love that once existed between Israelis and Palestinians over so many years, and put a stop to harm caused by either, against the other."

"We're with you, Esty," Khalib assured her.

"Thank you," she replied. "But from here on I must always be called Nura, not Esty. Hamas will likely give us some grace because of my name. And we need all the grace we can get as we move into the tunnels and encounter the militants along the way." She scanned their faces, each nodding in agreement.

"Okay, then," added Liyah. "Let's see if we can get in. We need to find a man named Hawk. Lead on Esty…I mean Nura."

Nura fixed her keffiyeh tighter across her mouth and led them down the main corridor, until they came to a sign hanging down from above, with an arrow pointing to the main door to the maintenance room. She began to push it open when Liyah grabbed her arm.

"Wait."

"What?"

Liyah slipped her phone from her pocket. "We need to leave a message for my parents…at least some encouragement that you, me, and Khalib are okay and that we'll check in again as soon as we can."

Liyah pressed her home phone number.

Nothing.

She tried again.

Still nothing.

She stared at the phone. "I'm not getting any signal at all…no bars."

"Let me try," said Nura. She removed her phone from her trench coat pocket and dialed Liyah's house.

Nothing.

She glanced at the battery indicator, then the signal strength. "I've got enough juice, but no signal either. I mean *none.* How weird. It's only a floor down. Should at least have something here."

Liyah looked back at her. "I'm worried. Not sure there'll be any connection in the tunnel."

"We don't have much choice, Liyah," replied Khalib. "We need to get moving if we're gonna work through these tunnels and get back before our parents lose their crap. And believe me, these tunnels can be rough, and confusing."

Liyah nodded to Nura, who pushed open the door.

They entered into an expansive room, housing the power generators for supplying electric, water, air conditioning, and ventilation services, as well as communications. The equipment hummed loudly, and multicolored lights blinked everywhere. They moved slowly along the main aisle until they approached a man bent over one of the generators, pushing down on a large wrench with both hands. He turned around as if mystically sensing their presence and rose.

He was a large man, both in height and weight. He wore torn baggy jeans that topped heavy leather work boots, and a tan, grease-smeared work shirt—the hospital logo above the pocket. A narrow black sweatband was wound around his head, balancing his black curly mustache. He studied the visitors, his eyes finally settling on Nura.

"Help you?" he asked, his voice serious, deep, and rough.

"Hawk?" asked Nura.

He tilted his head slightly but didn't answer.

"We were told to see you. To get access to the tunnel."

He remained silent for a moment before replying, keeping his eyes on Nura and ignoring Liyah. "I don't know what you're talking about."

"So you are Hawk, then," replied Nura.

"Why do you need to get in?"

"To meet with some important people," she lied. "We're part of a mission that involves the situation with the hostages."

"What people?"

"We can't say," she lied again.

"How old are you…and these lads here?" He glanced over at Khalib and his friends.

"What difference does it make? The project is secret. Do you know who I am?"

The man studied her. "Of course."

"Then?"

He placed the wrench on top of the generator. "This way."

They followed him to the end of the aisle, took a right turn, and walked down a series of narrow stairs. He began to open a door to a side room marked ***Danger - Keep Out***, then stopped. He pointed to Nura.

"Just you."

Nura looked at the others, then back at him. "They're with me."

"Sorry," he replied, his voice gruff, impatient.

Liyah stepped forward. Reaching into her jacket pocket, she pulled out a folded piece of paper and handed it to him. "Malik sent us."

He took the paper and opened it. His stiff expression eased. "So it's you. He did mention a few others would be along as well, but funny that he didn't mention Nura or that the boys would be just out of diapers."

Hawk studied them one more time before opening the door, then led them to the far wall of the room. Pushing away a drape, he uncovered an access door that looked like it might double as the entrance to a bank vault. He typed a code into the electronic panel. The heavy latch clicked. He pressed down hard on the lever and the door swung open.

As they stepped into the tunnel entrance, Liyah turned to him. "I'll need that paper back."

"No way," he replied. "Malik's orders were that no one is to know he's involved, so it stays with me. You're on your own."

As Liyah's eyes met his one last time, he reached into one of the deep pockets of his pants. "But these will help."

He pulled out a handful of what appeared to be coins and handed them to her. "One for each of you. They prove you came in legitimately. Don't lose them."

He yanked on the lever, closing the heavy door, until it clanked shut behind them.

Twenty-Seven

IT TOOK A while for Liyah's eyes to adjust to the dim light. As objects in the room slowly came into view, she grabbed hold of her friend's arm. "Crap, Es," she whispered, "What have we gotten ourselves into?"

Nura...only Nura when talking out loud."

"Yeah, okay. I never did like dark, enclosed places. Morningstar helped me get past that, but if I get caught by surprise, I seem to fall back into panic mode until I can take a few breaths and focus. At least there's a little light in here from that one bulb over there."

As Liyah took a few steps toward it, her toes hooked under something on the floor, nearly bringing her down. She pulled her shoe free, noticing it was a handle of some kind. She bent down, gripped it, and tried unsuccessfully to pull up.

"Guys," she called out to her brother and his friends. "Help me with this would you?"

Jawad reached her first and yanked on the handle, slightly lifting a panel that was set into the floor. A flash of light appeared briefly around the edges of the opening before he let go. The panel slammed shut.

Ali assisted him, and together they pulled the trapdoor up, resting it against the wall. Light poured up from below.

Liyah looked down. A sudden rush of fear grabbed hold of her chest and rose to her throat. She fought back at it. "The tunnel is a lot deeper than I expected."

"They need to be in order to be secure from tanks, bombs, and missiles," Khalib replied. "This is similar to the one at the old airport. We need to climb down this long, steep ladder here, so I'll go first with Ali, and we can help you and, ah, Nura. Jawad, you pull up the rear and close the trapdoor behind you. Pass down the packs first."

Once they were all safely at the bottom, they glanced around. The tunnel ran in only one direction, and where they stood was clearly the terminal point. It was shaped almost like a tube, and high enough to easily accommodate a person well over six feet tall; more than wide enough for a vehicle as well. The walls were covered with concrete tiles and piping. Intermittently spaced lightbulbs lit the way.

"What's next, Khalib?" asked Ali. "Looks like a pile of trouble ahead. No place to hide. Not sure what I was thinking."

"Ha!" Khalib snorted, smiling. "What else you got to do? This is fancier than the tunnels I was in—down south by the old airport, near the border with Egypt."

Jawad moved his fingers along one of the multiple sets of pipes that lined the wall on one side. "What are these for?"

"Power from the generators mostly, for lighting and communications, but also water and ventilation, " replied Khalib. "It's pretty musty down here, but at least there's air."

"What do you think, Nura?" asked Liyah. "Ready to move out?"

"No sense in standing here. We have a lot of ground to cover and little time."

They entered the tunnel, Liyah and Nura side by side followed by the boys. After walking for a half hour they came to two openings, directly across from each other. On one side was an archway that led to a giant storeroom and two other rooms. They stepped inside.

"Allah!" Jawad blurted out, as he walked next to rows of shelving holding hundreds of automatic weapons, guns, grenades, tens of thousands of rounds of ammo, clothing, and other assorted items…then past giant locked bins. "It's like a warehouse for war."

"Because it is," replied Khalib.

Ali peeked into one of the other rooms, to his right. "Two big generators in here. And a bunch of electrical panels."

Liyah stepped into the remaining room, then back out. "Bedroom here, with several bunks."

They crossed over to the other side of the tunnel and into another large room, well lit. On one end was a full kitchen, with cabinets, a small stove, shelving, a sink, refrigerator, and countertop appliances. In the middle of the room was a large table. Folding chairs were positioned around it and against the other wall. The five took seats around the table, setting their packs next to them.

Liyah unfolded a large piece of paper in the center of the table. "Kind of a crude map of Gaza, but I had to draw it myself in a hurry, after Ets…ah, Nura and I went into Gaza City to meet Ahmad's contact, Malik. I was certain then we were not going to avoid ending up in these tunnels. I also searched the Internet for all known information about them. Hamas tries to keep the locations completely secret. It works to a large degree, but you'd be surprised what you can piece together. The Israeli and other media even give up clues, unknowingly."

"Like what?" asked Nura.

Liyah pointed to the top of the map, where she had written the name of the town of Jabalia. "This is where we are now, near the refugee camp and the Al-Amal Hospital. The media tell us where all the recent shelling has been concentrated, and IDF is bombarding mosques, schools, hospitals, certain manufacturing facilities, etc., claiming that Hamas operatives are hiding in these places, or underneath them. As of right now, the IDF doesn't really know the extent of all of these tunnels, but they're finding out. Malik alluded to this by telling us there are hundreds of miles of tunnels and that most are interconnected."

"How does that help us?" asked Ali. "Seems like we're just as confused as the Israelis are."

"Because if you combine all these pieces of information and overlay them, you get something that looks like this." She pointed to marks she had made in different colors all over the map. "These in red are the mosques, these in blue the hospitals, green the factories, and so on. And to the east are where the Hamas attacks on Re'im and the other kibbutzim occurred. I made a rough draft like this first then drew lines connecting likely paths…shortest distances between all these places."

She looked up to make sure everyone was still listening.

"And?" prompted Khalib.

"And when you get an overlap of a lot of lines, they kind of make a pattern when you discard the lighter traffic lines. What you're left with is these lines in black and brown shown here." She moved her index finger along several. "The brown ones are shorter distances that connect individual buildings or locations to each other, or to the main tunnels. The ones in black are the probable main tunnels that run long distances…like the one we're in now and connect most of the other tunnels together."

Khalib nodded his head in approval. "That's genius, Liyah. "But we're still left with hundreds of miles of tunnels."

"I know," she replied. "But keep in mind that most of the heavily used tunnels are up right here in Gaza City or slightly south. And we only need to get some additional info to narrow down where Hanna is possibly being held."

"There are hundreds of hostages, though," Nura advised.

"But she would stand out," Liyah replied. "Many of the women were released recently, and the rest are almost all men from what anyone can tell. We only have to ask everyone we run into."

"Assuming none of these '*everyone's*' kill us first," Ali added, "when they find out we intend to help her escape."

"Just go along with this, will you guys? Jeez! What other choice do we have? At least this narrows it down. All we can do is do our best. It's a long shot anyway, and it will be hard to maintain our cover."

She pointed again at her crude map. "If you look at this you can see that the first main tunnel section is likely the one we're in. And we can follow this south, then either decide to continue toward Rafah, or shift to an area we think she might be."

Nura ran her finger along several of the possible tunnel routes. "What's the distance we're talking about?

"From here to a handful of the schools and mosques south of Gaza City it's about five miles or so. From there, east to the border near Israel, the direction where Hanna may have come from, it's another mile or two." Liyah took a deep breath. "But from here to Khan Unis it's over twenty miles, and to Rafah, near the southern border, almost twenty-five."

"Let's hope it's the former and not the latter," said Nura.

Khalib stood up. "And even at that we still have to assume we're not chasing Alice down a rabbit hole."

Liyah folded up the map and pointed over to the cabinets. "Fill up your extra water bottles here and see if there are some food supplies we can add to our own without weighing us down…and then let's move out. Fast."

Twenty-Eight

HANNA LURCHED FORWARD, reacting to the forceful push of a rifle butt against her back.

"Keep up, Miss Jew! You're lagging!" a guard grunted in his best English. He passed her by and made his way to the front of the pack.

Her legs ached and her mouth and throat felt as dry as the desert. She followed as close as she could behind Daniel, her shoes rubbing against the raw blisters on the sides of her feet and stinging unbearably with every step.

They had picked up a handful more hostages, all men, and several Hamas soldiers since the last stop for a mere sip of water. She counted a total of sixteen: four soldiers, all wearing black balaclavas, two head guards in full camo, and ten hostages—all men except for her. No one was allowed to speak as they moved slowly along stopping only after long intervals to allow a few people to use the cramped pit-stop areas carved into the side of the dirt and rock wall along the way.

She and her fellow hostages moved through the tunnel slowly, in single file and holding close to the wall, one guard at the front and one usually at the rear. The soldiers kept to their left, moving forward and back to occasionally check on them, and keep them from talking.

Hanna's mind drifted as they marched along. She was losing track of the days. *How long had it been since she saw daylight?* she wondered. *Where were her parents? How would anyone ever find her? Were they going to kill her? How might that happen? Rape? Torture? Starvation?*

She reeled her mind back in as they passed another one of the side tunnels that forked off both to the right and left every so often. The branches appeared slightly more narrow, maybe allowing a small car to pass but not a transport vehicle, she thought. She noticed markings on the wall at each intersection. *Perhaps some sort of Arabic etchings or code?*

The head guard yelled something out she couldn't quite decipher, and the soldiers then herded them all into another of the large storage areas off to the side. They were then all forced to sit cross-legged again along the semi-tiled wall next to the bins.

The guard stepped into the room, scanning his captives as he spoke. "You'll each be given some biscuits and water. You can go one at a time to do your business. We'll be waiting here for a while until some others join us. Make use of that time to rest. We still have a lot of ground to cover."

Hanna could see across the tunnel and into the room directly opposite. She noticed there was a big table, chairs, cupboards, and part of some kind of kitchen area over to the side. The soldiers and guards were gathering around the table, a few of them talking on their phones that operated within the special tunnel security system, several of the others chatted amongst themselves and laughed. Only one soldier remained in the tunnel between the two rooms, watching over them and alternately checking the tunnel in both directions. She poked Daniel in the side and whispered.

"Dan, I can't take this much longer."

"I know," he whispered back, keeping his eyes facing forward.

"Yesterday I overheard one of the soldiers say we were near some hospital north of Gaza City, and that there was a rumor of a possible hostage exchange. Then all of a sudden, we reversed direction and are headed back down this same tunnel. Doesn't give me a good feeling."

Daniel shifted his position, stretching out his legs for a moment then crossing them again. "There's not much we can do. We're really at their mercy. And I can't see any male my age making it out of here alive."

She turned to him. "Don't say that."

"It's true…And don't look at me. That soldier would just as soon bash us with his rifle."

She returned her stare to the wall across from them. "Still."

The main guard reentered the room and walked along the line of prisoners, stopping at her. He looked down at her. A chill ran up her spine.

"Ladies first," he said, his words void of any emotion.

"What?" Hanna replied.

"You heard me," he returned. "The loo is yours, around the corner. The soldier will show you." He then addressed the line of them. "Five minutes max in the loo. No exceptions."

She stood and followed the guard out of the storeroom. The soldier nodded to him and pointed the location of the room to Hanna. He followed her partway until she pushed through a door in the side of the tunnel and disappeared.

The stench in the cramped room overpowered her senses and burned her eyes. Her throat tightened to prevent her from gagging. A gap above the door provided enough light from the tunnel for her to locate the hole in the ground. Next to the hole, on either side of it, were short, tiled strips on which to place each of her feet.

Hanna positioned herself and undid her jeans, reaching into her underwear to retrieve the phone she kept hidden there, hoping the guards wouldn't find it. She then pulled her pants down the rest of the way and squatted over the hole. When she was done peeing, she wiped herself with the sleeve of her shirt and stood back up. She tapped the phone to get it to come alive then checked the power bar: maybe ten percent left, then the time: 4:05 a.m. She thumbed through the apps until she located the compass, knowing it would work even underground since it was subject only to the magnetic field of the earth. When she pointed it parallel to the tunnel, the direction they were headed in, it indicated *S*. She was satisfied they were headed away from Gaza City. *But to where?* she wondered.

She placed the phone in her underwear, pulled her pants the rest of the way up, buttoned them, and swung open the door to the tunnel.

TWENTY-NINE

A HORN BLARED, the sound echoing down the tunnel. Liyah and the others jerked their heads around then moved to one side of the tunnel and stopped, clinging closely to the wall. A handful of men in camo, most of them wearing black balaclavas, edged slowly by them in an open vehicle that looked like a Range Rover with open sides. The men sat with AK-47s at their sides, pointing straight up, and shouted profanities as they passed by. A short distance ahead, the vehicle halted.

The man next to the driver got out. He was the only one not wearing a balaclava but instead wore a round camo military cap. He approached them, scanning each up and down.

"What are you people doing in the tunnel?" the man asked, his face unreadable, his voice stern. "Who's in charge?"

They looked blankly at each other before Liyah stepped forward. "I guess I am," she replied, her voice unsure.

"You guess?" the man said. "And who might you be?

"My name is Liyah. Liyah Al-Rahim. We're from Beit Lahia. We're looking for someone."

"Where's your pass?"

"Pass?"

"Yes. Pass," the man replied, raising his voice.

"Ahh…"

"Here," said Khalib, disguised a bit by his balaclava. He reached into his pocket and then handed the man a coin.

The man studied it, flipping it from one side which bore the likeness of a golden eagle, to the other, and an embossed image of a key on the other—both Palestinian symbols. He returned it to Khalib, who, though many years his junior was slightly taller. "Where's your camo?"

"I still go to school," Khalib replied.

The man studied him again, then scanned the others. "Passes?"

Each dug into their pockets, eventually holding up the same coins Hawk had given Liyah to pass out.

He walked up to Nura, eyeing her leather trench coat and keffiyeh. "Are you with them?"

She nodded.

"That's Nura," Liyah interjected.

He looked at Liyah. "I know who she is," the man growled, before returning to Nura.

"Who are you looking for?"

Nura reached into her coat pocket and retrieved her phone. She thumbed quickly through her photos, showing him the image of Hanna she had shown to Malik.

"And?" the man asked, studying it.

"We need to find her, "Nura replied, her face showing relief he understood English. "We're on a special mission," she lied once more. "And this person is a prisoner."

"Who is giving the orders?"

"We can't say," she insisted. "But it's why we have these coins. Why Hawk let us by, and why *I'm* here." She moved her hand from the top of her black and white traditional keffiyeh, along her face, and down the full length of her trench coat, emphasizing her status.

The man stepped back, then studied the picture. "Where is she from?"

"Re'im."

He tugged at his long black beard as he looked back at Nura. "I see."

"Have you seen her?" asked Liyah.

"No. No one like that is in the tunnel."

Liyah felt uncertain he was telling the entire truth. She steadied her eyes on his and held up her palm to his face. Focusing her attention, she sent waves of energy at him, locking his mind on her, tightening his countenance, and mesmerizing him.

"How is that possible that you are one of the main gatekeepers and don't know? We feel she's definitely in the tunnels, so where might she be?"

"I really don't know for sure," he replied, succumbing to her will. "I heard they did take some people in from Re'im. They split them into groups, but she could have been one of those we were planning to release. That is, uh, until the IDF decided to cross the border with their army. We're now fighting them in Gaza, and many of the captives are being sent back south."

"Where are they going?" asked Nura.

"No idea. Maybe all the way to Rafah. But we all believe now that the Israelis will not stop until they get there, as well."

Liyah released her control of him. The taught muscles in his face relaxed noticeably.

The man blinked, then looked around as if he had lost his bearings. "My guess is somewhere off the main tunnel…either down by Khan Yunis or more east toward where she may have come from. I think they're holding them in small groups, out of the main traffic area where the IDF is likely to come looking first."

The man nodded to Nura. "I'd get out of the tunnel with your young friends if I were you. While you can. The Israeli soldiers are centering on the tunnels and want to obliterate all of us."

They watched as he got back into his vehicle and moved on ahead of them.

"What should we do?" Ali asked Liyah.

"No change in plan," she replied, glancing around at each of them. "I think that confirms we have only a few shots at finding her. Either before we get close to Khan Younis, because after that there are too many options where they may hide Hanna…or somewhere in the side tunnels that lead toward the eastern part of Gaza, out beyond the city limit."

She and Nura walked side by side, the boys following, as they moved farther south in the tunnel, passing by additional smaller tunnel branches joining from both sides and the occasional vehicle or small group of soldiers on foot. The soldiers often whistled and gave cat calls as they approached, becoming silent as the men passed by, turning their heads to stare at Nura, their mouths agape.

The five new comrades moved on, making frustratingly slow progress—stopped frequently by guards along the way and resting from time to time to refresh with sips of water. During some of the rest stops they shared bites of the nutrition bars and peanut butter from small plastic containers Liyah had distributed, along with the rolls, figs, and food they had taken from the tunnel kitchen.

About five miles in from their hospital starting point, after a full night without sleep, they neared what appeared to be a main intersection of some sort. Activity in the tunnel had picked up substantially. Liyah held her hand out to the others, halting their progress, then stepped toward her brother.

"Looks like there are a number of tunnels intersecting here. Can you, Ali, and Jawad scout around, then join us in what looks to be the main meeting area across the way there?" She checked the time on her phone. "It's getting toward morning. I think we're going to be forced to make a critical decision here. If we go too far down any of these tunnels, we might not have enough time left to check out a few more before someone figures out we don't actually belong here."

Khalib waved to his two friends who were looking at the markings at the intersection of two of the tunnels a few yards away. "Sure, Sis. Back in a flash."

As he and his friends disappeared into one of the side tunnels, Liyah and Nura walked a short distance ahead and into the kitchen area of the main tunnel.

THIRTY

"SWORDS OF IRON. It's a go," came the command to the Israeli commanders waiting across the border from the Gaza Strip. The highly anticipated land invasion of the Gaza Strip had begun. The brief eerie silence between the last round of artillery and bombing was broken as Israeli tanks, lined up along the northernmost border of the Strip, pushed forward toward Beit Lahia.

In the predawn hours and into the morning combat jets screamed overhead, and artillery fire peppered the small city of Beit Lahia and rained ruin down over the northern part of Gaza City. Missiles flew from the barrels of the sophisticated, heavily armed tanks, less than two miles from the outskirts of the city, and artillery fire intensified every hour. The bombardment destroyed targets presumed to be hiding places for Hamas agents, including schools, libraries, businesses, residences, and religious buildings.

The sky lit up with the light from the explosions, as the sounds of death exploded across Beit Lahia and moved further south toward Gaza City. Israel's Iron Dome defense easily handled counterattacks by Hamas missiles, as loudspeakers warned residents to clear out and head south for their own protection.

David Al-Rahim rocketed out of bed, pulled back the curtain, and peered out his bedroom window.

"Rania! Get up!"

She joined him at the window and glanced out over his shoulder. "Oh, Allah. What is happening?"

"Another attack. But this looks like the beginning of the invasion they've been talking about."

"What are we going to do, David?"

He took her by the hand. "I don't know. But we should probably get to the basement. C'mon."

"Wait. Let me at least get some clothes on."

"All right. I'll change quickly, too. And I need to find the satellite phone. My cell doesn't seem to be working."

After eventually making their way to the first floor, Rania took several bottles of water from the refrigerator and placed them in a cloth shopping bag along with some nutrition bars, fruit, cheese, bread, and crackers. Her husband continued to search for his satellite phone, rummaging through the drawers of his desk in the den.

"Got it!" he yelled as he made his way to the kitchen. "Let's go."

He turned on the light switch at the top of the stairs and led them down to the small finished part of the basement. They sat next to each other on the beige love seat and stared at each other.

"Oh, David," she said hugging his arm and resting her head on his shoulder.

"I know. I know."

"The kids are not back," she said, raising her eyes to meet his.

"Yeah. I've been up half the night. And I checked their rooms when I was running around looking for my phone. I guess they never came home at all."

His wife began to weep softly. He held her, then gently slipped away from her grasp. "I've got to try to call Liyah. I think this phone should work okay. Haven't used it in a while. My battery may be low on the cell." He dialed her number and put the phone to his ear.

"There's nothing. Very odd. The backlight works on this phone, and it seems to work okay otherwise."

He tried his son. "Same thing for Khalib. What the hell?"

"Maybe their phones can't get the satellite signal?"

"I don't think that's the problem. This phone can reach the satellites from anywhere, where there's no regular cell signal, then from there, it goes back through the standard communications infrastructure. Let me try one other to make sure this phone is not the problem."

He checked the contacts on his cell, typed a number into the satellite phone, and waited.

"Hello?"

"Hello, Adam?"

"Yes, David. We must have been cut off before."

"Yeah, sorry. I'm having trouble communicating with people and thought I'd try you on this satellite phone I use for the Dawn in case of emergencies or restricted calls. So this seems fine."

"Glad I could help. Anything else?"

"Yes. While I have you, I've got some not-so-good news, Adam."

"What's that, my friend?" he replied, his voice suddenly sober.

"We're under attack."

"What?"

"It looks like the border has been breached and the army has launched the ground war…I can see the tanks in the distance from the windows on the second floor."

"No!"

"Yes. But what's perhaps worse is the kids never came home last night."

"Come again?"

"Liyah and Khalib. And Esty. I haven't seen them since I came home last night."

"It makes sense now, David. I understand why you can't reach them."

"How's that?"

"The IDF was planning a blackout if they started an invasion. Cut out all communications within Gaza via land phone, cell, or whatever to protect the troops. They can do that because they control almost the entire infrastructure there. The cell towers must be blocked, so you won't be able to use the phones."

"Well, that means we're literally in the dark in trying to reach the kids, or vice versa."

"Seems like it," Esty's dad replied. "But where do you suppose they are?"

"Not sure, but where would you be looking for someone kidnapped from Re'im?"

"Tunnels?"

"Unfortunately. Where else?"

Both men grew quiet. The silence was finally broken by Esty's dad.

"You need to get out, David. Besides, there's something I need you for. I mentioned it earlier. I can't say anything about it over the phone, but your problems with the Dawn got me thinking more about it. I have already completed some of the plans."

"How would I ever get there with what's happening now?"

"You have my car, and that will help. And I've made arrangements with the Minister of the Interior to notify all the border stations to be on the lookout for you, and any passengers you might have…to let you through. You should bring your whole family and stay with Esty and me until it's safe to go back."

"That's generous, Adam, but I have to wait for the kids."

"I'm not sure you're going to be able to do that, David. I think they're on their own until the communications network is back up. And that may not be for months. Trust me."

"Allah!"

"Indeed," replied Esty's dad. "Call me back when you've had time to digest this. You know our daughters. I think they're actually stronger than we are." He forced a weak laugh. "We have to trust them. And on our side do everything we can to support them. We will have to use our connections and influence to correct this grave injustice our leaders have thrust upon the Palestinian and Israeli people. We'll chat later. But don't wait too long."

Liyah's dad ended the call and sighed, turning to his wife.

"I only heard one side of that, dear," she said. "But it didn't sound good."

"It wasn't," he replied, reaching for her hand. "We have some decisions to make. And none of them seem very promising."

Thirty-One

LIYAH AND NURA sat at a small table in the corner of the kitchen area, anxiously waiting for the boys to return. A dozen or so soldiers congregated around the large table in the center of the room, while workers buzzed about: bringing new items for storage, tending to pipes beneath the sink, checking fuses in the electrical boxes, and testing a newly installed generator that apparently supported the appliances as well as communications within the tunnels. The men were constantly holding their phones to their ears and then fidgeting with the panels above the generator.

Every now and then some of the soldiers would glance over at them. Nura had her back to the center of the room, unable to catch most of the stares, except when she looked to her side. Liyah glared back at one of the men directly across from her, who quickly averted his eyes after noticing hers.

"These guys make me nervous, Es."

"Nura."

"Sorry…Nura," Liyah whispered. "You're definitely the main attraction, though. They barely make eye contact with me."

"I think a lot of that is because my picture has been all over the papers the last year or so, because I visit some of the hospitals when I can, and the journalists are blowing me up into some sort of heroine to Palestinians."

"Well, you are Nura. I've read lots of those articles. I'm surprised they don't come over here to get your autograph."

"That wouldn't be too good, Liyah, would it? I mean we've been lucky I haven't been pressed to speak Arabic. Besides, I think it's kind of like some of the Hollywood actors in America...people are not certain that I might be who they think I am, and that keeps them at a distance."

"I hope that continues. I don't want to have to start anything. We're really trapped down here because we don't know how to get out, and we're outnumbered regardless."

"I know. I think..."

"Back in one piece," Khalib announced, pulling up a chair beside them. Ali and Jawad remained standing.

"Hush," Nura scolded under her breath. "You're drawing attention."

"You've been gone a while. I was getting worried. Some of these guys are more than creepy, and the two of us stick out like a sore thumb."

"Nobody bothered us at all. There are plenty of other Palestinian boys here even younger than us. And with the balaclavas, we don't even get a second look. I'm not sure we'll run into as many people as you might think down here who will question why we're here...that is until our cover is blown."

"What do you mean?" asked Liyah.

I mean that we will definitely run into groups of these militant Hamas guys, but you'd be surprised how spread out they are. With over five hundred miles of tunnels, the density of people can get pretty spread out. And they are mostly used for supplies and moving small groups around. As long as we stay together as much as possible, and don't cause any disturbances, we can increase our chances of being left alone. And don't forget, these other groups down here have their own missions they're concentrating on. What I learned from being in these tunnels six months ago was that getting in here in the first place was the toughest thing, but once you're in they don't question anybody much. But like I say, if our cover ever is compromised...well, then it's a new game."

Liyah nodded. "I see. So, what did you find out?"

"We checked out all the side tunnels nearby…about five altogether. Definitely more traffic than before, so something must be going down. We looked into all the storerooms and meeting rooms we could find. Three of them held some people who appeared to be hostages, with a couple of guards overseeing each of the groups."

"Any sign of Hanna?"

"No women at all." Khalib looked up at his friends and they nodded in agreement.

Nura sighed heavily. She offered Kalib her phone with the picture of Hanna on the screen. "Can you take this around to the men in here and ask them if they know where she might be being held?"

"If they want to know why, just make up some excuse, Khalib" added Liyah. "Tell them some commander wanted you to ask around. Act like it's no big deal."

"Easy for you to say…"

"Please," his sister begged. "Nura and I don't want to take a chance, and if you go alone no one is likely to suspect you."

He held eye contact a moment with her, then took the phone from Nura and began circulating through the room.

Ali grabbed several of the water bottles, filled them from the faucet in the sink, and brought them back. "Not sure how good this water is," he said, passing them out. "Israel controls most of the infrastructure, including the water systems, and has either shut them down or destroyed the pumps with the bombing. Saltwater is also seeping into the sources. It's getting bad."

Khalib made the rounds and returned after about fifteen minutes.

"Anything?" asked Liyah as he approached the table.

"Maybe, Khalib replied. "They pretty much believe most all of the women were let go during the first cease-fire. One of the workers did disagree with that, though. He said a group of hostages, I guess Hamas calls them prisoners now, were led down the tunnel a few hours ago and he thought he might have seen a woman with them, but he didn't get a clear view."

"Which tunnel?" Nura pressed.

"The one on the right as you go out of here. It's a pretty big tunnel, but he told me there were a lot of other offshoots to that tunnel as well. He said the one to a big mosque southeast of Gaza City was his best guess, but he didn't know how to describe the way to get there through the tunnels. Because there are no signs, and he hadn't actually been there before."

Liyah picked up her pack from the back of her chair and slung it over her back as she addressed the others.

"Time to go! Might be our only chance to find Hanna."

THIRTY-TWO

THE SOUND OF rumbling tanks, artillery, and small weapons fire closed in on Beit Lahia, the first major town in the path of the assault. Rania squeezed her husband's hand tighter.

"David, what's going to happen to us? Are they going to kill us?"

"I wish I knew," he replied, sounding defeated. "Although they're mainly after the Hamas terrorists and weapons stores…along with freeing the hostages. We have nothing for them."

"But we're in the path, aren't we?"

"Yes, unfortunately. There's not much we can do. We have to hope they'll center on the places where Hamas is hiding." His eyes widened the moment he completed the last sentence. His mind began to race. *The kids!*

'What about the tunnels?" He blurted out, unconscious that he was speaking.

"Tunnels, dear? What are you talking about?"

"Oh…nothing," he replied, catching himself. "Wondering about something, that's all. Just thinking out…"

WHAM!

An explosion nearby shook the house to its foundation, followed by the dull roar of tanks on either side of them, and the clatter of their treads as they moved along the paved streets.

"David!" his wife screamed in horror.

He jumped up and led her by the hand to the archway between the two sections of the basement. "This is the safest place we can be."

The rattle of the tanks and gunfire, interspersed with the thunder of jets passing overhead, lasted only about thirty minutes, but it seemed like a lifetime to David. All the time he thought about his daughter, son, and Esty. His mind raced once more. *They could be trapped in the tunnels. Or killed—collateral damage of the invasion.* And there was nothing he could do about it.

As the noise of the tanks and gunfire moved south toward Jabalia and Gaza City, he glanced at his wife. Her face was frozen in fear. He held his finger to his lips.

"Shh. It's okay…Wait here. I'll check things out upstairs."

"No, David! she pleaded. "Don't leave me here by myself."

"You'll be fine," he reassured her. "I need to see."

He left her and made his way up to the kitchen. The sound of the tanks was fading, but the distant echoes of artillery and gunfire persisted. He gazed through the windows at the smoke-filled air. Several homes in the neighborhood had been leveled to the ground, and another was standing but on fire.

He raced through the house checking for any damage but found none. He peered out all the windows, aghast at the broad devastation surrounding him. For an instant he felt lucky, then he thought of those in the homes close by, less fortunate…maybe even dead. And then Liyah, Esty, and Khalib.

At the top of the stairs to the basement, he yelled down. "Come up, Rania! It's passed!"

She ran to the top of the stairs and flung her arms around him. In the kitchen, she viewed the same scene he had, stunned and speechless.

"Come, let's talk," he said softly, leading her into the dining room. He took his seat at the head of the table. She sat at the corner next to him, silent, her eyes moist.

"Oh, David."

He reached for her hand. "We need to make some decisions now."

"Which decisions?"

"When I spoke with Adam, he was very concerned. I know you sensed that from my part of the conversation. But the bottom line is that he knew this was going to definitely happen, he just wasn't sure when. That's why he was pushing for Esty to come home."

"What does that have to do with us? What decision are you talking about?"

He squeezed her hand gently. "Let me finish, dear. Adam offered to help us leave Gaza…and go stay with him and Esty at their place outside of Jerusalem. He's arranging for us to be able to pass through the border. We have his car. It will help, and we can leave at any time. I think we need to get out now before it's too late."

He watched his wife's expression turn from mostly fear and anxiety to one more calm, but serious.

"We can't do that, David. What about the children?"

"I fear they are trapped in the tunnels now, or at best will not be coming home soon," he replied. "All communications have been shut down in Gaza by the IDF. There is no way to reach them. Adam wants my help in something important which I believe relates to all that is going on. I have to see what I can do to keep hope alive for all Palestinians, not just my family…but I can bring you with me. When we locate the kids, Adam will be able to help get them to safety."

"We can't do that," his wife insisted. "We can't leave here. It's our home."

"It's only going to get worse." He looked into her eyes. "Adam knows this, and so do I. I need to see what he has in mind, and we can decide to return when the primary danger is over. A lot of people are going to die here needlessly."

"They're already dying, David, from the artillery and missile strikes over the past weeks. Thousands of innocent people…and children. The hospitals are getting overrun, water supplies are drying up and food is getting more scarce."

"That's exactly what I'm talking about, Rania. And it's going to get much worse before this ends."

"How can we ever leave our children?"

"We're trapped, dear. But I feel that it must be done. They are strong. Adam even said they are better equipped than we are to survive in this current environment. They have grown up very fast this past year, you know that…all the trauma we have all gone through, but especially them. They'll be fine. We will see them again."

"How can you be so sure? I feel we would be abandoning them."

"I'm as sure as I can be, Rania. I am useless here now, at least until the press starts up again if that ever happens. Perhaps I can do something with Adam, and we can return soon."

She sat quietly for a minute, holding on to his hand with both of hers before letting go with one and bringing it up to his face, caressing his cheek.

Okay, dear. I understand. I do. But I will not be going. I will be of no use there. If I stay here, I can help care for the injured children. I thought about this already…after Amina bandaged you and told us about the shortage of help at the hospitals. I can be of service."

"But…"

"I'll be fine, like you said. The house is still in one piece. If the kids come home, they will have a place to stay until we can figure out the next steps. I'll be here for them. I'm sure Adam can find a way for us to keep track of each other."

He gazed into her eyes, wondering why he had never witnessed this strength in her before. *I have always cared deeply for her,* he said to himself, *but perhaps I had not given her the chance to show me this side. We were raising the kids, and it was tough at times…and then I was busy at the paper. Had I shortchanged her all these years? When was the last time I told her how I truly felt?*

"David?"

"I love you, Rania."

Thirty-Three

NURA PULLED HER phone from her pocket as they made their way through the tunnel. Her feet ached and even the leather coat couldn't prevent the straps of her pack from digging into her shoulders, forcing her to constantly readjust it. She removed it and set it down. The others stopped along with her, making use of the time to drink some water and grab some snacks.

"We've probably gone about a mile down this one, and nothing," Liyah complained, holding her arms out to the side to signal her frustration.

"Yeah," Nura agreed. "It's past noon and all we've seen is a few small groups of soldiers in some of the cutout storerooms along the way. We've been down here for about twelve hours. Even if we find Hanna, I'm not sure we're ever going to find our way out."

As they rested, sitting in a line with their backs resting against the tiled wall, Liyah pulled the map from her pack and unfolded it on her lap. Her brother and Nura sat on either side of her. She placed the compass of her phone on top of the map.

"I'm thinking we're somewhere near here." She pointed to an area near the edge of the city, where she had marked several mosques with small red circles. "It's about a mile southeast of the city, which aligns with the compass…only a short distance from where we are now. The outermost mosque is the largest, and might be the place where they could be moving many of the hostages to."

"We don't know which tunnel will bring us there," Khalib cautioned.

"Probably the one to the left according to your map, Liyah," added Nura.

Liyah traced her finger along the map. "Could be. It would make sense, but then…" She sighed and folded the map back up. "Let's move on. We're close enough to take the chance of asking someone. Must be another meeting area up ahead soon."

After a short fifteen-minute walk they approached another intersection where the tunnel they were in met two others. Two of the tunnels, theirs and the one to the left, were smaller than the main tunnel they had been on earlier, but large enough to allow small vehicles to pass. The third, to the right, was too narrow.

Nura pointed to the fork to the left, where several soldiers gathered around three open-top vehicles. The Jeep-like vehicles were parked in a row, pointed up the tunnel, away from them.

"Looks like some major activity."

"I'd say so," Liyah agreed. She took a deep breath. "Must be the meeting area. Let's join them."

Nura cast her a look of trepidation but nodded her ascent and signaled the boys to join them. The entrance to the room was just beyond the third vehicle. They passed the main group of soldiers, then squeezed past the vehicles. The soldiers paid no attention to the boys in their black balaclavas but a number stopped talking and stared at both Nura and Liyah as they walked by.

The room was similar to the other kitchen areas with the shelving, sink, and tables. The tables were fully occupied so they gathered together in the corner of the room, next to one of the generators.

Khalib walked over to the main table and said something to a worker sitting at the near end. The man nodded. As Khalib returned to the others, one of the soldiers, wearing a circular cap, followed him with his eyes.

"What did you say to that man?" his sister asked him.

"I pointed in the direction of this tunnel and asked if that was the way to the mosque. It is."

Nura smiled at him. "Good work."

"Well it doesn't mean she's there," he replied, "but we may be a step closer."

"This place makes me nervous," Liyah said. "Let's each take a bathroom break in one of those hideous loos and be on our way before something happens."

"Okay," agreed Khalib. "Ali, Jawad, and I can stand guard while you two go first. It'll look less suspicious that way. They seem to always have a guard present when hostages are involved. So maybe they'll think we're watching over you."

As they moved toward the exit, Khalib asked one of the soldiers the location of the loo. He then led the others out of the room, back to the intersection of the tunnels and a short way up the tunnel they had already been on.

"Here it is," Khalib offered to Liyah, apologetic, but winking his eye. "You're room is ready, ma'am."

Liyah shook her head and chuckled. "Some things never change, do they?"

She held the door for Nura then followed her into the dimly lit, gross-smelling room. Khalib heard their muffled gasps and complaints to each other as they closed the door behind them.

A few minutes later they emerged, and the boys began to each take a turn. Ali went first, the other two remaining with the girls as guards. Nura glanced slightly up ahead and across the tunnel at another opening. Two guards stood out front, chatting. She turned to Khalib.

"Do you mind walking me over there?" She pointed to where the guards stood, just to the side of the opening of the room.

"What for?"

"There must be some hostages in there. I can check it out, but they'd be suspicious if someone looking like you wasn't with me."

Khalib laughed. "Even you…Nura?"

"Why take a chance?" she replied, her eyes narrow, her mouth stern.

"Got it," he replied, matching her seriousness, then leading her over to the guards.

One of the guards had his back to them as they approached but turned around after seeing the expression on his fellow soldier's face. Khalib stopped in front of them. Nura moved up to his side.

Khalib nodded to them. "Excuse me. We're looking for someone…a prisoner. It has to do with the hostage deal headquarters is working on."

"Are you…?" the closest guard began to ask, not finishing his sentence.

"Yes," she replied, matter-of-factly.

"She's here as part of the negotiations," Khalib responded. "We need to verify that one of the prisoners is still alive."

"Which one?" asked the other guard.

"She'll know him when she sees him," Khalib replied. "It's all legit."

Nura nodded in agreement.

The guards hesitated, looking at each other then back at the both of them.

"Well…we assume that. But procedures…you understand."

Nura pulled the coin from her pocket and handed it to the guard. Khalib then did the same, adding "We entered the tunnel at the far end under the Al-Amal Hospital. A man named Malik paved the way. And a fellow named Hawk…"

"I know of Malik but not this person…this Hawk. The coins are enough." He faced Nura. "You can go in but make it quick."

She stepped into the dimly lit room. Khalib began to follow but was stopped when the guard pushed his rifle against his chest, blocking his way.

"One at a time," the guard insisted, locking eyes with him.

She scanned the room after her eyes had adjusted, estimating maybe a dozen men sitting along the walls. She walked slowly, a few yards or so from them, allowing them to continue their whispered conversations, or simply glance at her as she moved along, not wanting to call attention to her. Nura looked down at each as she passed by, close enough to see the light reflecting off their faces.

As she neared the last few, her heart sank, like it did each time she had done this through the journey inside the tunnel. She was running out of time and options, and she knew it.

Nura turned her attention to the last two hostages, separated from the others, sitting facing each other near the corner of the room. She moved closer. One of them with a scruffy beard looked up. *Certainly could pass as Jewish like the others,* she thought. She shifted her eyes to the one he was whispering to.

The face finally came into focus. Nura studied it. Her mind went into overdrive. She shifted her eyes rapidly back and forth between the face and the headscarf that bordered it. *A girl? No! Not any girl. Hanna!*

Tears swept into the corners of Nura's eyes. She wiped them away with a flap of the keffiyeh that covered her forehead. She stifled her reflex to yell for joy. Instead, she squatted down in front of her friend. Touching her fingers to Hanna's lips, she used her other hand to pull the keffiyeh from her mouth and chin. Then smiled.

Hanna's eyes flew open like saucers.

THIRTY-FOUR

"ESTY!" CRIED HANNA, her voice muffled quickly by Nura's hand.

"Shh. You need to call me Nura, okay? Or none of us will get out of here." She removed her hand. "And no emotion. No nothing. Got it?"

Hanna nodded. She touched Daniel on his knee. "He's got to come, too. His name is Daniel."

Khalib caught up to Nura. "The guard sent me to retrieve you. No more time."

Nura studied Hanna and Daniel. "Okay. Not a word, you two, when we take you out of here," she said under her breath. "This is Khalib, and there are others with us."

Daniel nodded but whispered back. "We'll need to take the middle tunnel out of here."

"How do you know that?" asked Khalib.

"You know the symbols embedded and scratched into the wall at the intersections, the squares, triangles, stars, and all?"

"Yeah. We did notice them, but we couldn't figure out if they were important."

"So, each of the tunnels is represented by one of the symbols. We were blindfolded when we were kidnapped but these symbols act like a coded map to a subway system. Instead of colors, they use the symbols, and the endpoints of each tunnel by other characters, so you know what direction you're going in. Distances are in kilometers, and are simply represented by numbers."

"Okay then," Nura said. "But we can't do this right now. It won't work. We'll have to leave you, but we'll return."

Hanna's eyes pleaded with her.

"I know how you feel. But sit still and be quiet. We'll be back."

She stood up and signaled to Khalib. They walked slowly across the room and into the tunnel. Khalib thanked the guards in Arabic then led Nura back to the others by the loo. Jawad, the last to use the room except for Khalib, was closing the door.

"Any luck?" asked Liyah.

"She's in there," Nura said, her voice urgent.

"Hanna? Where?"

"There's another storage area across the way, like the others we've seen. She's in there, with a guy named Daniel and about ten other hostages. She wants him to come out with her."

"I don't know, Nura. This is going to be impossible as it is. Another person to be responsible for…"

"He's got to come with us, Liyah," Khalib insisted. "He knows how to get out."

"Okay. How many soldiers, including guards, do you think there are?"

He thought for a moment, counting on his fingers. "I'd say about eight in the kitchen area not counting the workers, a handful out by the cars, and two at the place where they're holding Hanna…so maybe fifteen altogether that could give us trouble."

"Those aren't great odds for us," Nura replied.

"Keep in mind we had some advantages," Liyah reminded her.

"Seriously?" Ali questioned, sarcastically doubtful. "Like what?"

"Just follow our lead," Liyah replied. "You and Jawad will need to steal a few weapons when you have the chance. Nura will team up with Khalib, they've been in a similar situation when we rescued Khalib last spring and fought off the terrorist attempt to destroy Jerusalem. I'll try to maximize the distractions and work some magic."

"Magic?" questioned Jawad.

"Keep the faith, Jawad. Throwing rocks won't work in this situation. But as a team, we can make it out of here."

"We need to act fast, Sis. What can we do?

Liyah studied the anxious faces around her. She pointed to her brother and Nura. "You two. You need to go back and get Hanna and her friend, Daniel. Make up some lame excuse, but bring them to the main intersection of the three tunnels. I'll distract the soldiers by the Jeeps in the far tunnel that are pointed in the direction of the mosque. Nura, do you think you can keep anyone from exiting the kitchen storage room? Create a magnetic field to block them."

"Yes, I think I can. I've been practicing with the energy, like did in Jerusalem."

"Energy? Magnetic fields? Oh, Allah," Ali moaned. "Now I know we're in trouble."

Liyah held out her hand. "I need all of your passes…the tokens."

One by one they dug into their pockets, retrieved the coins, and laid them in her palm.

Liyah turned to Nura. "Here. We'll take our chances from here on out. Since you can speak Hebrew, give these to five of the hostages, and tell them to pair up with the others. If there are guards outside, maybe they'll let them pass if they say some of them were lost. It's worth a try even if it's a long shot. We will protect the rear until we exit the tunnel. The signal for them to run toward us will be an explosion."

She faced Khalib. "When Nura is in with the hostages, you're to keep the two guards occupied. Ask them if they've heard any news about the IDF breaking into the tunnel or something. When Nura joins you with Daniel and Hanna, start to walk toward us. Nura can turn and freeze them in their tracks while Ali and Jawad take their weapons."

"What!" exclaimed Jawad. "Freeze, then jump them? Are you kidding?"

"Just go with it Jawad. We'll only get one shot."

"Now," Liyah continued, "I'll stand at the intersection. "While Ali and Jawad keep the two guards from moving, Nura, you, and Khalib will join me. You need to move past the vehicles to the front of the kitchen storeroom opening and secure it. Khalib will stay with me. We'll distract the soldiers hanging out near the intersection. Once you've set up the field, Nura, you need to join us quickly. The field won't last long."

"Got it," Nura replied.

"Lastly," Liyah added, looking around at them, "once Nura joins me and Khalib, I'll set off the signal. The hostages will run out of their room, joining Ali and Jawad. And so will we, all of us heading up the middle tunnel as fast as we can." She took a deep breath. "Any questions?"

Liyah glanced at the dumbfounded expression on the faces of both Ali and Jawad. "Good. Now let's make it happen!"

As Nura and her brother made their way back toward the hostages, Ali and Jawad followed a short distance behind, looking like Hamas citizen soldiers themselves in their black balaclavas. Nura and Khalib spoke with the guards for a few minutes, then Nura entered the room where Hanna and Daniel were waiting, leaving Khalib with the guards.

Nura bent down to Hanna and Daniel, going over the details of what was about to happen. Next, she moved down the line of hostages, handing out the coins to every other hostage, and repeating the instructions each time. She then returned to her friend, signaling her and Daniel to stand.

"Okay. This is it. No going back."

She hugged Hanna, then led the two of them past the other hostages, and out of the room.

She passed by the guards without acknowledging them, Hanna and Daniel in tow, headed toward the intersection. One of the guards turned from Khalib, toward her.

"Wait!" he yelled to her.

Nura grabbed hold of her half-heart necklace and turned as Khalib stepped aside. She pointed her other hand in the direction of the guards and focused her mind. A stream of bright white light poured from her fingertips, striking both, stunning them. Ali and Jawad ran up to Khalib, helping him overpower the guards, stripping them of their weapons and two grenades. While the guards slowly tried to recover, Ali and Jawad pointed the rifles at them.

Khalib caught up to Nura, right before she reached the intersection of the tunnels. Liyah was waiting there. He remained with Hanna and Daniel while Nura made her way up the far tunnel, past the vehicles, and to the kitchen. Liyah stepped toward the soldiers hanging around by the Jeep nearest to the intersection. She paused before moving any closer, keeping her eye on Nura.

Nura opened the door and entered the kitchen area. A number of the men turned their heads to her. She stood motionless for a minute, bowing her head, focusing her mind, gathering her strength.

More faces turned.

She raised both arms, holding her palms outward.

Still more faces turned, studying her, wondering.

Nura brought her eyes up, staring blankly toward them, then let go a force that filled the room, freezing everyone in place, like statues. She backed out of the room and into the tunnel, turned, and headed toward Liyah, alongside the parked vehicles.

When Liyah saw her coming she stepped closer to the group of soldiers. Once Nura was by her side, safely past the Jeep closest to the intersection, she clutched the jewel around her neck, faced the Jeep, and sent a beam of laser red light at its tank.

As one of the soldiers pointed toward her, yelling a warning to the others, the tank blew apart in a massive explosion that engulfed the vehicle in flames. Liyah then turned to the men and fired beams of energy at their weapons, heating up their rifles instantaneously, causing them to glow bright red, forcing them to throw the weapons to the ground and hold onto their hands, screaming in pain.

The explosion had signaled the hostages. They poured from their room into the tunnel. Liyah signaled to Nura and they both ran toward the intersection. As they approached, Liyah yelled toward Daniel, breathing hard.

"Which way out?"

"Back up the middle tunnel," he shouted back. "Follow me!"

The five hurried back up to where Ali and Jawad held the guards, and the hostages had collected.

Daniel pointed up the tunnel. "This way. Hurry." He started walking quickly then broke into a slow jog. The hostages followed. Ali and Jawad let the still groggy soldiers go but kept their rifles, hustling down the tunnel behind the hostages, trailed by Hanna, Nura, and Khalib, with Liyah only a few steps behind.

The two guards recovered, running back to the intersection to join their comrades. One of the men who had yelled slurs at Hanna before was barking orders, trying to put out the fire in the Jeep, and using the middle Jeep to back into it and push it out of the way. In the meantime, they were trapped.

Khalib caught up to Daniel as they all hurried through the tunnel. About fifteen minutes later they came to another fork in the tunnel. Stopping there, they waited for the others to arrive.

Having finally freed the other two Jeeps, soldiers backed them out of the intersection, loaded in as many men as they could, and began moving up the middle tunnel, the remaining soldiers trailing behind on foot.

After everyone had arrived at the fork, Khalib approached Daniel. "Which way do we go from here?"

"The markings on the wall indicate we should keep to the left. I have a feeling that all the other tunnels off of this one will not be wide enough for car traffic, so that means this is the main way out. We need to stay on this one to the end.

Although we were all blindfolded when we entered the tunnel from the Israel border, I heard car engines. So I'm assuming this will be right."

"Any idea how far?" asked Khalib.

"Can't be very. If I'm correct, we've already gone about a half mile…possibly only fifteen more minutes if we can keep the pace."

"Well, I do hope you're right. We can't keep up this pace with a big group like this. And we don't want to leave anyone behind if we don't absolutely have to."

Daniel gave him the thumbs up. "Agreed."

"Let's move out then."

Khalib signaled to Nura, and they started herding everyone along.

Ten minutes later Liyah began to feel a rumbling under her feet, then the sound of an engine perked her ears. Last in line, she halted. She felt her heart race as she waited, silent, holding her breath while she listened intently and stared back at a bend in the tunnel. The sound grew louder until suddenly the beams from headlights appeared on the tiled wall near the bend.

Liyah ran to catch up with the others, yelling.

"Step on it! Let's go! No stragglers!"

They all started running, pushing themselves, and using up whatever strength remained. The first Jeep rounded the turn, catching them in the beams of the headlights. The leader yelled out more orders. The Jeeps accelerated and the soldiers began running behind, closing in on their targets.

"Move it! Faster! shouted Khalib, turning around to encourage them. When he turned back, he could see the tunnel start to slant upward.

Daniel approached him. "The end is not far away, Khalib. I remember this. It will lead up to gates."

"Keep them going, Daniel. I've got to fall back and help Liyah."

As the hostages—depleted from being held captive underground with minimal food—struggled against the increasing steepness of the tunnel, Khalib passed by Ali and Jawad, motioning them to follow. Liyah stopped running when she saw them coming.

"We need to hold them here," she called out as they joined her.

"It won't last for long, Liyah," Khalib replied. "They have grenade launchers on those Jeeps and plenty of automatic rifles. We won't be able to get close enough to stop them. We're outnumbered."

"I'll stay here with these two. You head back and keep them all together. They're gonna need help if there are guards at the entrance."

"Okay…but get your ass out of here before it's too late."

"Don't worry about *me*. Get going."

As Khalib started running back to the others, gunfire from the Jeeps rang out, spraying bullets in their direction, and ricocheting off the walls.

"I need them to be closer to be effective," Liyah shouted to Ali and Jawad. "You guys start giving it back to them. Make them think twice, and slow down."

"Aye, aye, captain!" Ali replied. "I've used one of these before at a practice range." He aimed and squeezed hard on the trigger, blasting thirty rounds down the tunnel at the soldiers.

Jawad tried the same, but unfamiliar with the AK-47, sent bullets flying wildly along the tunnel, the kick from the butt of the gun bruising his shoulder. "Damn!" he yelled as he tried again and again, increasing his accuracy.

The fire from the two guns briefly silenced the soldiers as they took cover. The Jeeps stopped for a minute then began moving again. A soldier in the lead Jeep mounted a grenade launcher on the top of his shoulder and fired.

Liyah saw a puff of smoke and heard the thump of the grenade exiting the barrel. She held up her hand and sent a band of energy in the general direction. The grenade exploded about fifty yards from her and the boys, the shrapnel from it hitting them with only light force, unable to puncture their skin.

Ali and Jawad continued firing, silencing them once more.

"We can't stay here, Liyah yelled. "We've slowed them down but we may not survive another exchange like that. Let's go!"

They turned and began running to catch up with the others. The first group of hostages had already made it to the end of the tunnel, a large space with several vehicles parked to the side. A glass guardhouse and two metal gates blocked their escape. Two guards stepped from the guardhouse that was built into the inside part of the entrance and confronted the group. Another guard remained inside.

The hostages, along with Nura, Hanna, Daniel, and Khalib approached the two guards, and the paired hostages presented the coins to them.

"There's not enough to go around here," said one of the guards. "Where did you get these?"

"We lost some," Khalib replied, thinking, trying to buy time.

Nura looked down the tunnel ramp. The figures of Liyah and the boys began to appear. She turned back toward the guard and stepped forward.

"They're with me. We're on a mission."

"Nura?" asked a guard.

"Yes."

"What's going on here?

"Nothing," she replied, trying to distract them longer. She signaled Khalib with her finger to come closer to her.

Gunfire rang out inside the tunnel from the soldiers.

Both guards jumped, then stared down the ramp, seeing the Jeeps in pursuit of Liyah, Ali, and Jawad, who were now only a short distance away.

"What the…?" stammered one of the guards, incredulous.

The other guard, caught in confusion. studied the two boys with Liyah, both wearing black balaclavas and carrying

AK-47s, then Khalib, also wearing a balaclava. "What's going on?" He demanded.

Suddenly the guardhouse door flew open and the third guard stepped out on the platform. "The Commander of Fifth Tunnel Brigade is on the line. He's ordered us to stop this group!" he shouted.

Nura latched onto Khalib's arm with one hand and yelled at him. "This is like Jerusalem. Concentrate! We'll combine our energies. Grab that guy's arm and don't let go!"

Khalib did as ordered, reaching out and grasping the guard's forearm, while Nura pointed at the other guard. Electric shocks shot through the two men, their rifles dropping to the ground.

Khalib bent down and picked up the rifles, keeping one and handing the other to Daniel. They stepped back and pointed the barrels at both guards.

From the tower, the third guard shouldered his rifle and pulled back the lever on the top of the gun. He released a spray of bullets that hit the tunnel near Daniel.

Liyah had caught up, and before he could get another round off, a red beam from her fingers found the rifle and blew it out of his hands. She pressed through the crowd and approached the gates. Holding her hand up toward the huge steel latch, she melted it into molten jelly, releasing the gates.

Khalib, Ali, and Jawad then helped Liyah swing the heavy gates open, as the panicked hostages wedged their way past. Gunfire hit the roof of the tunnel above the gates as the soldiers closed in.

"Everyone…through the gates!" Liyah shouted. "Run! Keep Running and don't stop!"

She turned to Nura. "Stay by me. I need you." She glanced up at the rock face where the tunnel exited. "Let's bring it down."

After everyone was a safe distance from the gate, the two of them slipped out as well.

"We need to be close enough to maintain power," Liyah reminded Nura.

The Jeeps and soldiers neared the top of the ramp, firing their rifles, and waiting for another opening to use the grenade launchers.

"Now!" Shouted Liyah.

Both girls pointed to the rock ledge above the tunnel ceiling and focused their attention. An avalanche of small rocks began to break off the surface and fall to the ground inside the tunnel. The earth shook near the guardhouse. Then, with a deafening roar, the entire side of the rock ledge above collapsed, blocking the advance of the soldiers and sealing the tunnel.

The girls brought their arms down and stared at each other. Liyah tapped her friend on her shoulder and smiled.

"Like old times, wouldn't you say, Es?"

Thirty-Five

IT WAS LATE afternoon when Liyah's father called Adam Blum on his satellite phone. Esty's dad answered after one ring.

"David! I could tell it was you from the number. I've been worried about you and your family. Must be hell there."

"Hi, Adam. Hell would be a vacation."

"I'm so sorry, David. Truly. Hate seems to be the operative word these days."

"Yes. We had Israeli soldiers running through our backyard firing indiscriminately, and there is massive destruction all around. People are dying by the hundreds it seems, every hour. Men, women, and children...even babies. The attacks by Hamas on the kibbutzim have unleashed the pent-up frustration on both sides, but we're the ones who are paying for it...not Hamas, and not your government. It's worse than I've ever seen it in my lifetime, and I fear there may be no going back this time."

"That's why I need you here, David. I believe there's a road to a better future. I can't have you getting killed there. Your even-handed treatment of the conflict over the years is appreciated by both Israelis and Palestinians, even if the extremists on both sides oppose you. And personally, I feel strongly that we need to move away from the path we are on. Others in the government will join me, but we can't afford to waste any time and miss this window where I have the approval of the Prime Minister. He's bound to change his mind when he figures out that our success will ultimately lead to his own demise."

"Can you tell me more about the project itself?", asked David.

"I've gotten the approval of the government to work on a special peace initiative, but it needs involvement from both sides and centers on the media. It won't stop what's happening now, but it is a path for the future. I'll be able to tell you more when you get here. There's a very tight window to get it going, held together only by the Prime Minister's ego and desire to look like he's working for peace, when in fact he isn't. Are you still coming? Have you heard from the girls?"

"No, unfortunately still no word. Cable news is still working here and I see that the IDF is targeting the tunnels, mosques, and even hospitals, looking for the hostages. I'm deathly afraid the kids are trapped. And I'm not sure I'll be able to get out of here, regardless. They've blocked all the roads."

"I've cleared the way for you. We can make it happen. There's nothing we can do right now about the kids, like we said. Grab Rania and come as soon as you can, before it gets even worse."

"Rania declined. It's a long story for a later time."

"I still need you, David. You can do more here than there, I assure you. The Ministry of the Interior is in charge of all passes. They are aware that you will be coming, along with possibly your family and my daughter. The IDF is also aware. Along with the documents in the glove box that Esty uses to get around, there is a special code and two telephone numbers that will get you directly through to the right people at the Interior or the Prime Minister's office."

David hesitated. "Will I be able to get back?"

"Yes, yes. Of course, David. And this is only temporary. Once everything is set up here. The operation can be run from anywhere, even if most of the staff is here."

"Okay, Adam. I'll give it a try. Where should I meet you?"

"I'll text the directions along with the code and phone numbers right after we hang up. You can use your cell phone here, but I'd bring both just in case."

"Will do."

"See you, David."

The text arrived in a few minutes. He copied down the information on a piece of paper just in case, then gazed out through the broken glass of the dining room windows. With the main assault force already cutting its way past Gaza City and heading south to Khan Younis, the sound of gunfire had departed Beit Lahia. The last explosion he had heard occurred several hours ago, in the distance. Outside the fall sun shone brightly between two slowly drifting puffy clouds, and a light breeze made itself present in the leaves of the olive trees.

It was as if the beginning of the war was only some kind of a dream, and he would soon wake up.

Thirty-Six

HANNA'S FIRST INCLINATION was to not stop running, ever. But when she looked back over her shoulder, no one was following her. She stopped. They were standing, talking, about forty yards beyond the gates. There wasn't a soul around. Esty turned around and yelled at her.

"Hold on, Hanna! We're trying to get our bearings."

She walked back to the group as Liyah handed her cell phone to Daniel. "Here's the compass, Daniel. You might be the only one who knows where we are."

"Dan is fine, Liyah. Call me either."

Liyah grinned. "Okay…Dan."

Hanna was struck by her smile. Other than the fleeting moment of joy she felt when Esty unveiled herself, she couldn't remember a moment of happiness for some time. Ever since the raid of horror at Re'im.

Dan glanced at the compass, then scanned the area. "This entrance to the tunnel is really well hidden. It faces south, toward a vast area of nothing. They've built up dunes around here to disguise it."

The hostages milled about in a confused aimless state as Dan made his way to the top of one of the sand hills next to the tunnel entrance, scouted the area, and then returned to the group.

"I think I know where we are. I kind of suspected if we made it out of the tunnel alive we'd likely end up somewhere around here." He pointed toward the dune he had climbed up. "That's due north. From up top there you can see a complex of industrial buildings in the distance. Part of it is an environmental project for solar energy. The team I was on for the archaeological dig when I was picked up was allowed to go there for a day to get supplies and see the project."

He turned and pointed in the opposite direction. "Straight across this barren stretch is the border with Israel…less than a mile away. I was by myself with one other person. I don't know what happened to him. We got surprised, and I was hit on the head. Next thing I knew I was walking down the ramp, blindfolded.

"How are we gonna get out of here?" asked Esty.

"Well, my car is parked only a few hundred yards into Israel, a fairly easy walk from here, if it's still there. But I can only fit four in it."

"We have to get Hanna back to her parents first. How far is Re'im?"

"Only about four miles or so from the border. It would be a long walk, but doable if the car's not there."

"I suggest we get Hanna back, like you said, then take Esty home," replied Liyah. "She wouldn't do well trying to get back up through the Strip if the formal invasion has begun. And they've been sending artillery and missiles into Gaza City and other places for weeks now. It's dangerous. Plus with her being Jewish…the way things are. You know? I don't know how long she'd get away with being Nura."

"Yeah," Khalib added. "You lose whether you're an Israeli or a Palestinian right now in Gaza…and she's both." He chuckled, then caught himself. "Well, you know what I mean."

"Sad, but true," replied Dan. "I'd be worried, even for an American like me."

"So, what I'm suggesting," continued Liyah, "is that Khalib, Ali, and Jawad head back to let my parents know we're okay. I think you boys will be fine, Khalib, you have your balaclavas in case Hamas harasses you, and you know how to take the side alleys to avoid the Israeli soldiers who would probably be coming down the main streets if they've started."

"We'll be all right," agreed Khalib, "but how do we get from here to some place we might recognize?"

"Just head right toward that industrial park you can see from the dune I walked up," replied Dan, and keep going north. In a few miles, you'll be on the outskirts of Gaza City."

"I'm good from there," Ali assured Khalib."

"The hostages," said Jawad. "What about them?"

"They can follow us to the fence. To freedom. Then we can hustle to my car. It's not far. We can let the authorities know where they are so they can pick them up." He turned to Liyah. "And how about you? We have enough room, you know."

"And I could drive you back home once we reach my house near Jerusalem," Esty added.

"You're forgetting your dad's car is at my house."

"Oops, yeah, well my father will get you home safely for sure. And I'd love to have you visit anyway. I don't know when we'll be able to do it again."

"All right," agreed Liyah. "Do you mind Khalib?"

"Not at all. I think you'd be safer now that way, even if you wouldn't be with us tough guys to protect you." He laughed. "Kidding, but no one is safe now in Gaza."

They checked their packs to even out the water and snacks. Ali and Jawad said their goodbyes and began walking up the dune. Khalib hugged his sister and Esty then nodded to Hanna and shook hands with Dan.

"Keep them safe."

"You bet, Khalib. I have a feeling all our paths will cross again."

Khalib started up after his friends when Hanna caught him from behind and grabbed his arm to stop him.

"I wanted to thank you personally, Khalib. Esty told me how she and Liyah tease you a lot, but that you have been there for them whenever they asked. And that you brought Ali and Jawad into this dangerous rescue attempt with you."

Tears filled her eyes and she kissed him on his cheek. "I see what you are all trying to do to change the future. I want to be part of that. Please stay safe and help your friends get home in one piece."

"I will, Hanna. Thanks for that." He saluted her, his seriousness melting into a warm grin. Then he turned to join the others.

Thirty-Seven

DAVID AL-RAHIM turned into the parking lot not too far from the Jaffa Gate entrance to the Old City section of Jerusalem. Esty's dad was waiting at the entrance. He put down the driver's window as he pulled to the curb in front of him.

"I'd recognize that car anywhere," Adam joked, pointing to the Ministry sticker at the corner of the windshield.

David shook his hand through the open window. "Hello, Adam. I'll swing this into that open space over there and be right back."

Adam gave him the thumbs up and waited. When David returned, they made their way up the street and through the great stone archway that marked the entrance to the Old City, the home of some of the holiest of sites to Jews, Muslims, and Christians alike. In a few minutes, they stood before the great carved wood doors that led into the Church of the Holy Sepulchre, located in the Christian Quarter of the city, the sacred site where Jesus was crucified, and where his tomb resides.

Immediately upon entering the church, Adam led them down the stone steps into the basement. The tapping of their shoes echoed through the narrow hall as they passed several small, sequestered chapels and then stopped. Adam lifted a key from his pocket, placed it into the keyhole of a small wooden door, and turned it. The door opened into a surprisingly good-sized room. They stepped inside.

"This is what I was telling you about on the walk up here, David. Not many people know about this room. I found out about it from Esty. She knows the place inside and out from the tours she does here and in the Muslim and Jewish Quarters." He laughed. "I sometimes wonder if the Pope even knows about this."

David scanned the room, noting the modern tables, equipment, and furniture filling the space—computers, in-baskets, and phones arranged like a high-tech company in Silicon Valley in America; chrome swivel desk chairs on castors; extra-wide video screens mounted to the old stone walls; and two large electronic whiteboards at either end of the room.

"This place is the safest in all of Israel and Palestine, David. Not only do very few people know about it, but it's protected by the holiness of this site, and I have the buy-in from the Muslims who hold the actual key to the site, the Jews—or really Israelis, who run all of Jerusalem including the Old City, the three Christian groups that run this church, and even the Prime Minister."

Adam set himself down in one of the chairs.

David followed suit, sitting on the corner of one of the tables. "You said you wanted to set up a media center, but what exactly do you mean by that…and why here?"

"Simple. You and I have had several discussions on the topic of the conflicts here in this part of the world, the Levant as it was always called. We met thanks to our kids, and thanks again to them we came to a greater realization of the need to step back, away from the confusion of today's politics and religious extremism and try to imagine the Levant in a new way. I was thinking we made some progress last spring…right here in the Old City. Remember?"

"Yes. I certainly do."

"But that is already being threatened by this *war*. The region is being set back a long way as the extreme elements on both sides kill any chance of lasting peace and foster hate between both sides. It's because the only way they win or keep power is to do that very thing: drive both sides further apart, using fear and a corrupted view of religion, or the state as their weapons."

"Well, you know we see eye to eye on this," David replied. "But I fear that the Israeli leaders and the Palestinian leaders will never see the error in their ways, and we can't solve the problem for the long term if they don't."

"Exactly, David."

Adam pushed his chair from the table, riding it until the castors stopped rolling. He stood up and started pacing in front of the whiteboard. "That's what I mean. *They're* the real problem! Not *us*, and not the average Israeli or Palestinian. We are waiting for leaders to solve the problems here because the average person, on either side feels powerless. Yet these *leaders* are not *our* leaders if you know what I mean. They do not see the light, the light as our own children have already explained to us. They don't understand the underpinnings of their own religion and have co-opted it to serve themselves and their own egos and use it against others. They don't see the common spiritual connection of all religions. They don't want the people to have any power at all. The whole thing has to be flipped."

"Flipped?"

Adam sped up his pacing.

"Yes, flipped,' he continued. "The power must be taken away from them and given back to the people. There was a time when all the people of the Levant were brothers and sisters. They cared for each other. Even Jesus, Mohammed, and Moses were brothers under Abraham, over two thousand years ago."

"I agree, Adam. Liyah told me that this mystical person she refers to as Ooray has passed this very message to her and her friends."

"I've heard something similar from Esty, too. Although I'm at a loss about this Ooray. I guess I haven't spent enough time with Esty to find out more about what she's talking about."

"So, what are you proposing, Adam?"

"I'm not proposing, David. We're *doing.* This idea has been brewing in my head for a while, but with this threat of the invasion of Gaza, I knew it was now or never. Esty told me about this place but isn't aware yet that I've done anything. It all happened in the last week. I secured the room and then my relation with the Prime Minister allowed me to get things done quickly, so I had the tech guys in the Ministry hook this all together the last few days.

"Why are the religious heads in the Old City, from the three religions, helping?"

"Because they see their own vulnerability. If this city blows up they lose everything…maybe even their lives. True religious leaders know that love, kindness, and compassion are the pillars of each religion—not the crowns, robes, and incantations. The founders: Jesus, Mohammed, and Moses, were simple men with simple messages, belief in others, and a sense of something bigger than themselves. Peace, true peace, is the only thing that can shelter them and make their flock safe. That is what I promised them, and also what I asked of them…to lead by helping us broadcast these messages."

"How did you get the Prime Minister to agree to this?"

Adam sat back down in his desk chair. "Well, to tell you the truth, I'm a bit disappointed in some policies he supports that I hoped I could help change."

"Like?"

"Like the encroachment of the settlements into the West Bank that are pushing the Palestinians out; the control of most all Gaza infrastructure which we are now using against them, even as hospitals are bombed and people starve; and the failure to speed supplies and medicine to the embattled civilians while the IDF tries to rout Hamas."

"Why do you think he supports those things? You know him pretty well, don't you?"

"Indeed, I do, David. He's older than me, but I got to know him when he and I were in America pursuing degrees. He was bright, hardworking, and driven. We both had interests in business, technology, and politics. He hired me to help as an advisor…sort of a roving ambassador but without the baggage of being an actual one, to keep an eye on international relations and help him navigate those complicated and troubled waters."

"What happened? Did you have a falling out?"

"I wouldn't say that, exactly. He supports this project I am working on because he sees the need to calm the Israeli people and keep his standing as their leader, by still providing a free press. And he sees the value of social media in his power struggle. It's that I don't think he sees the real truth about how some of his actions actually promote the hatred I'm talking about, just like the actions of Hamas do. They lead to even more instability over the long run…serving no one."

Adam pursed his lips as if trying to push back against a sense of anger rising in him and continued. "It's his ego, I believe. Power and money corrupt by playing on the egos of weak leaders. They can never get enough, and in that sense, I have had some disagreements with him lately, but he still values my service and sees the importance of having someone like you be part of this. I think you can see why, at least as an *appearance* to him."

"Only because I'm Palestinian and he wants it to look like he's trying," David replied, his serious tone matching his friend's.

"That could be likely, David. But he also admires you, personally, and there's no sense in cutting off our noses to spite our faces. He has now blessed this, and the equipment is here. Our job is to provide the truth for the region, whether he or Hamas likes it or not. Hasn't that been your life's mission all these years?"

"Yes. It has."

"Then let's get started. He won't be able to stop this. He doesn't own the Old City and we have the religious factions backing us, too."

"You're sly like a fox, Adam."

Adam winked. "It's our time."

"But what about Hamas, Adam? They are likely to cause more trouble in the Old City, here, to further divide the Israeli and Palestinian people. After all, they named their attack on the kibbutz *Al-Aqsa*, after the great mosque right across the square from this church."

"Yes, you're right. They're a problem for sure. But I have faith that any trouble they cause in Jerusalem will be overcome by the vast majority of people of all faiths and ethnicities here, who are sick of them and other extremists, who want peace—to live side by side, in harmony. That is the truth. It is how our ancestors lived…throughout the ages. It's up to us, and our kids, to help secure it again."

A broad smile returned to David's face. "So, do you have a goal in mind? Any rules?"

"The only goal is for you to run a successful operation. Since you're the journalist and have already built a successful media company before, I have full confidence in the success of this project. But I was thinking maybe we should make it more of a *new* media project, you know—social media focused. More targeted to various audiences. Plus, no need to print a paper."

David nodded. "Yes. I think that would be more efficient, and able to fly under the radar as they say. No one would need to know where the headquarters are. And we could reach more people, not only in Israel and Palestine but around the world."

"Exactly. And with regard to rules…I see only one guiding principle."

"Which is?"

"Using the truth to overcome fear and seed hope. This is the only way to remove the power from the grasp of the extremists, undercut their egos, and engage the public to cleanse the corruption and hate from the Levant…once and for all.

"What got you going on this in the first place?"

Adam took a deep breath. "Well, our daughters have been educating us, don't you think?"

David laughed. "Yeah. And it's their future, isn't it?"

"But also, I still believe there's a role for the leaders of every country to play in making a better future for all people. I'm happy to contribute on that end in my role as a consultant. But the more I get exposed to the inner workings and goals of certain political groups, like Hamas and the extremists in my own country, the more I see the danger…and the more I shift to the belief that the biggest engine for change and future happiness has to come from everyone. From the ground up—in our capacity as humans. We must look out for each other and stop the hateful, egocentric leaders that drive wedges between us. It's on us all."

David left his perch on the corner of the table, nodding his agreement. He grabbed a marker from under the paper flipboard that was positioned next to the whiteboard.

"As you were talking, Adam, you triggered a thought in my aging brain." With bold strokes, he wrote on the board.

The Levant Light

Adam reached out and shook his hand. "Welcome aboard."

THIRTY-EIGHT

THE AFTERNOON WAS waning. Dan and the girls walked along next to the high barbed wire fence that was swirled like a giant Slinky, separating southern Israel from Gaza.

Dan pointed. "I see it just up ahead."

"The car?" Liyah replied, squinting her eyes. "I don't see it."

"No. The hole they cut in the fence they used to carry out part of the raids. The one they used to kidnap me, and other hostages, too."

Dan led them through the gap in the fence, and into Israel. A short distance later they located the car he had left there when he was working on the university dig. He fiddled under the fender and pulled out a metal case that had been magnetically attached to the frame above the wheel.

"Got it," he said. "Let's hope it starts."

He slipped the key from its case and pressed the button twice. All four latches clicked. He opened the driver's door and slipped in, inserted the key, and twisted it. The engine started without any hesitation.

"Jump in! Sorry for the mess. Just push the tools and other crap out of the way. This isn't the newest car and the battery has seen its day. I think we got lucky."

Liyah took the seat next to Dan, with Esty and Hanna in the back. As they pulled away, Dan pointed to a group of large rocks off to the left. "Those stones mark the dig site. We had just begun to search for human remains that might have signaled an early path taken by humans thousands of years ago."

"Hanna told me you're from America, Dan. Where?"

"I'm actually staying in a dorm here at the university in Jerusalem at the moment. But my family lives outside of Boston, in a town called Newton. Fortunately, they don't even know I've been missing."

After a short time, the car left the hard-packed dirt road they had been on the last two miles and bounced onto a paved surface.

"Back in civilization, as they say," Dan declared. "This is the main road that will take us to Re'im. I bet you're anxious to get home, Hanna."

"Yeah. For sure. How far?"

"Only another few miles. You should have cell coverage from here."

Hanna took her phone from her pack and clicked on her home number. Esty tried her home as well.

"No one's home," Hanna said. "Maybe they're still at work."

Esty set her phone on her lap. "No answer for me either. But I don't dare bother my dad at work, he's probably there working overtime as usual."

"Well, don't worry," Dan replied. "We're almost to Re'im anyway, and Jerusalem is only a few hours from there."

Hanna gazed out the window, finally recognizing where she was. "There's a fork ahead, Dan. Can you swing into the campground where they held the Supernova festival?"

"Are you sure you want to do that? I mean…memories and all."

"I remembered that my parents were going to pick me up there. I just need to know if…" Her throat tightened up.

"Sure, Hanna. I'm sure everything's okay. I don't know why anyone would still be there."

"I just need to do it," Hanna replied. "For a couple of reasons. Did you know the theme of the festival was love and peace?"

"Yes, I knew that. How tragic that hate showed up as well." He turned the wheel and entered the road to the festival, driving past the campground.

"Allah," Liyah said, staring out her window. "Stuff is still around, scattered everywhere."

"Looks like they're still investigating, as well," Esty added. "All the taped areas, and police wandering around.

Dan drove past what used to be the stage area, now only a few broken tables left, along with random plastic bags and trash scattered about.

Hanna's mind began to flash back again. The memories she had pushed out came flooding back in.

"Stop the car, Dan," Esty said, gently but firmly as possible.

He pulled to the side of the road and looked back at her, then Hanna, who was staring out the window motionless, pale as a ghost.

Esty placed her hand on Hanna's leg and tapped lightly. "Hanna…Hanna."

Hanna finally turned to her "It was awful," she mumbled, grabbing hold of her friend's hand. "There was the sound of missiles and hand grenades exploding nearby. No one knew what was going on. Then people on motorbikes and in vehicles raced in from all sides, firing machine guns. People started to scream and run around in panic. You could hear the sound of bullets hitting parked cars, the tent poles, and the speakers on the stage. People started dropping like flies. I ran toward the exit and saw one girl try to get in her car. They shot her leg clean off. The next guy through looked down at her and then shot her in the head."

"Jesus!" said Dan. "I had no real idea it was that bad."

"It was worse," replied Hanna. "It was a war zone. But one side had no weapons at all. It was a slaughter."

"All right. That's too much for you now, Hanna," Dan replied. "Let's get you home. I'll swing along this row of cars up here and head back to the main road.

As Dan passed the cars, he noticed that most were damaged, many riddled with bullet holes, or blown apart. "Look at the damage those guys from Hamas caused. It may take months to clean up this place and remove everything."

Hanna collected herself and glanced out the window. "Wait! Stop!" She yelled. "Up ahead there!"

"Where?" asked Liyah.

"By the light blue car. Stop there."

Dan put his foot on the brakes and pulled behind the car. Hanna pushed open her door and flew out of the car. Dan got out and joined her.

"What's up, Hanna?"

"This is my dad's car."

"Really?"

"Yeah. But look at it. There are bullet holes in the passenger door and the windshield is shattered." She paused, and her face went pale. "I feel sick to my stomach. I need to get home, Dan."

They jumped back in the car and made their way out to the road and back to the fork. Hanna directed Dan and within ten minutes they were driving down Hanna's street.

"Three houses up on the right, Dan."

As he slowed down, he noticed a few of the houses on the street had yellow police tape blocking the driveway. Hanna's was one. He parked at the curb near the mailbox, behind another car with a man sitting in the driver's seat.

Hanna jumped out and ran to the front door. They all watched as Hanna read the sign on the door and then began to open it. But a man inside pulled it open the rest of the way. He and Hanna appeared to have a brief conversation, then Hanna screamed and fell onto the stoop before the man could grab hold of her.

Liyah flung open her door and raced to the house. She helped the man lift her as Esty and Dan arrived.

"What's happening?" Dan asked the man. "Are you her dad?"

"No," he replied. "I'm part of the police, an investigator, here checking on a few things. I had to inform her that her parents were shot to death at the festival. We've been looking for their daughter. We've been looking for *her*."

"Oh God, Hanna!" cried Esty, wrapping her arms around her. "Oh, God."

THIRTY-NINE

ESTY HAD CHANGED back into her street clothes when they stopped at a station for gas, stuffing the trench coat and keffiyeh into her pack. Hanna was now fast asleep, her head resting against Esty's shoulder. Esty pressed her forehead against the window, staring out toward the horizon, watching the setting sun as it tried to once again fight for its life.

Liyah fought to keep her eyes open but finally conceded to her overwhelming tiredness. Her head drooped forward, and her breathing became heavy. Dan looked over, smiled, and then checked his GPS app. *Not long to go.*

Liyah's face twitched several times, and her throat tried to speak, emitting only a low guttural sound. But in her mind, she was fully awake. She had traveled through space to some far-distant planet. Ooray appeared in front of her, like before—a vague multi-colored spectral form. Ooray's voice was calm and soothing, moderate in pitch. Neither male nor female. She recalled again the mission she had been sent on less than a year ago.

"Liyah. The time has come. Look at the people you have already reached and those whom you have now engaged to set fire to the chain reaction that will ultimately bring love and peace to humanity…starting here in your homeland. The birthplace of civilization.

The stars are aligning. The darkness has arrived again, but it is that darkness that comes before the dawn. You must help the others see this. You must use what special powers you have to light the way, always knowing that in the end, they are only the initial flash of the explosion.

The avalanche that will occur will come from the masses of people, all focused on helping each other."

"I know, Ooray. I will try harder. I will not disappoint you."

"You could never disappoint me, Liyah. You only have to share the beauty inside you with others…then believe in them. But there is one special thing I want you to do tomorrow. The hospital where Ahmad is has been hit by a missile. I want you to go there and bring Esty with you. Let her see that he is all right before news of the attack reaches her. And let your mother and brother know you are all right as well."

Ooray's image sputtered, then faded away, and Liyah awoke.

Dan glanced over at her. "That must have been some dream you had. You were talking in your sleep. Who the hell is Ooray?"

Liyah logged the essence of the dream in the back of her mind as she returned to the living. "Oh, uh…yeah. I'll fill you in later. Looks like we're just about there. Take a left under the second lamppost up ahead. Her house is the first one on the right."

Dan laughed. "We still have to talk about some of that other stuff that happened during the escape, too," he said, finally turning the car into the driveway.

Liyah looked over at him and smiled.

The darkness had set in, but small white outdoor lamps lit the path along the walkway to the house.

"You can park in that small turnaround, next to the garage," Esty whispered from the back seat.

He turned off the car, stepped out, and opened the door next to Hanna while Liyah opened Esty's. He eased Hanna out as she slowly awakened. She looked up and hugged him, pressing her head against his chest.

Esty and Liyah led the way toward the front door. They passed Esty's dad's car, parked near the front gate. "Interesting," said Liyah, pointing to the sticker on the windshield.

"I'd say so," Esty agreed. "That's a surprise."

Liyah breathed in the fresh fall air as the four mounted the steps to the front door. "I love it here, Es."

Esty put her hand on Hanna's shoulder. "This will be your home, too, Hanna, until everything gets sorted out." She pressed down on the latch and pushed open the heavy door.

They entered the foyer. Esty took Liyah's pack from her and placed it on a hook next to hers, then led everyone down the hall and into the den.

Esty's dad turned around when he saw the surprised look on David's face.

"Esty!" He stood up, stepped toward her, hugged her tightly, then kissed her on her forehead. "I've been telling Liyah's dad here that you'd both be fine, right David?"

Liyah's dad was halfway across the room when Liyah met him and gave him a great bear hug. "Oh, Baba. I thought I might never see you and Mama again."

"I'm so relieved, sweetie. Your mother will be glad to know you're safe."

"Where is she?"

"Still in Gaza. I'll explain later."

"Oh, excuse me," said Esty. "Intros! Dad, you remember Hanna, I'm sure. And this is Daniel."

He stepped forward. "Yes, of course, Hanna. It's been a while. And hello Daniel…nice to meet you." They shook hands.

"Nice to meet you, too, sir."

"And this is Liyah's dad," Esty added. "I'm sure you've gathered that by now."

He stepped over to Hanna and Dan, shaking their hands.

"We had dinner already, but there are some leftovers and snacks in the fridge. Hope it's enough."

"Dad, can I talk to you privately for a minute?" Esty asked.

"Don't worry, Es," Liyah replied. "I'll get the food out of the fridge and put it on the table. Let's all go get situated in the dining room."

Esty and her dad remained in the den while the others made their way toward the kitchen. She closed the door and took a seat on the small couch. He sat in his favorite chair."

"Something up, Esty?"

"We escaped the tunnels and ended up near where Hanna had gotten kidnapped…in Re'im. We stopped by her house a few hours ago and found out her parents were killed in that attack. She has no one. I told her she could stay with us until we figure everything out."

"Oh, dear. Yes, yes, of course. That would be the least we can do. I noticed her eyes were a bit red and she looked tired."

"She slept all the way here, but I know she's in shock. That's how I felt when we lost Mom."

"Right, well, you're all safe now so we'll concentrate on that. What about the young man?"

"That's Daniel. He goes by either that or Dan. He's in college in Jerusalem but lives in America. He got us from the tunnel to here."

"Okay. Let's go join them. So much is happening. Lots to talk about."

The food was already spread out on the dining room table, along with glasses of water, plates, forks, and small paper dinner napkins, when they entered. Her dad took his usual seat at the head of the table, opposite Liyah's. Esty sat next to Hanna, across from Dan and Liyah.

"This is quite the surprise, everyone," Esty's dad announced, holding up his water glass. "It's nice to have you safe…Cheers!"

Tears poured instantly out of Hanna's eyes and down her face like a waterfall.

Esty frowned at her father.

"Oh, I'm so sorry, Hanna. I didn't. I mean I…"

"It's all right, Dr. Blum," replied Hanna stuttering through her sobs. "It's not your fault."

Esty's dad reached behind his chair. He brought the two silver candlesticks and a pack of matches from the top of the bureau back to the table. He handed them to his daughter and nodded. Then addressed Hanna.

"This is a tradition in our house, Hanna. Every night Esty lights the first candle in remembrance of her mom, my wife, so that she is present with us. We then use her candle to light all the others. In this case, tonight, we have only two candles. We would like you to do the honors. To light a candle for your parents, and then use that one to light the other, so that Esty's mom can join us, too."

Esty passed the matches to Hanna and moved the candles closer.

"Go ahead, Hanna," she whispered. "It will help you, and all of us."

Hanna hesitantly took the matches, opened the flap, and struck one of the matches. Her hand trembled slightly as she brought the flame to the wick of the first candle. When the flame caught, she blew out the match and then turned to Esty.

"Go ahead," Esty prompted again. "I light this candle for…"

Hanna studied her friend's eyes, then glanced around the table. A few tears began to trickle.

"I light this candle for my mom and dad, who loved me so much. I never told them I knew that. I hardly ever told them how much I loved them, too. I'm telling them now."

The tears poured down, but she was able to keep her composure enough to continue. "They showed me what love is. They were always there for me. They never hated anyone."

She turned to face Esty. "And my friend here, next to me, has also taught me that everyone deserves to live in love, and in peace. That these desperate times are not the fault of those who truly believe in kindness and forgiveness…and live for each other. My mother and father are no longer here not because of Palestinians, but because of those who are blind, and simply live for themselves. We all know who they are. They are present on both sides. It is them I blame for this."

Her voice started to falter. "I miss them terribly already." She looked down, gathering herself, then picked up the candlestick and held the flame to the other candle until the new flame held.

"I am honored to bring Esty's mom to the table by lighting her candle. My parents are honored by this as well. I know this because they are with me now. It is their hands that now steady mine."

Her tears poured forth again. She used a napkin to wipe them dry, then continued.

"I want to thank Daniel for being there with me in the tunnel. He made me braver than I thought I could be. My heart is also with Liyah, her brother, and the others who came to my rescue, and the rescue of the other hostages. They all risked their lives. But above all, I want to thank Esty for never giving up on me. For being more than a true friend. She told me recently this broken world would be fixed if we simply put others first. She has done that for me always. I think she and Liyah are the living truth of that notion."

Esty reached out and touched her arm. "We love you, Hanna."

Hanna broke into tears again, hugging her. She looked across the table at Liyah and smiled through her tears. "And I saw some things during that escape that still need explaining, I'll have you know."

Liyah laughed. "Yes. That's what my dad says to me all the time now."

"Enjoy what food we have here, everyone." Esty's dad said. "David…I mean Liyah's dad…and I, have been up to something. That's why he's here. Go ahead, David."

"What?"

"Tell them. I mean there's no sense in secrets with this group. Tell them about The Levant Light."

Liyah's dad went on to explain the ideas behind the new media company and its focus. Esty's dad ended with an invitation to everyone to come into the Old City to see where the office was located.

"That sounds great," said Hanna. "I haven't been there for some time."

"She also happens to be a whiz with social media," added Esty.

Adam applauded. "Well, there you go, David. Our first employee."

They sat around the table eating and chatting and telling their rescue stories. Whenever the subject came up with weird lasers, melting guns, or magical jewelry Liyah would change the subject.

Dan finally excused himself, noting that he'd be in Jerusalem anyway the next day and they should call him when they arrived.

The two men stayed to talk in the den, while Esty showed Hanna to the small spare bedroom, then joined Liyah who was waiting in hers. Liyah was already in bed. She closed the door, took off her clothes, turned out the light, and slipped into the other single bed next to Liyah's.

Liyah waited until Esty had stopped gently thrashing, like a dog twirling to find the most comfortable position to sleep.

"Es."

"Oh, I thought you were already asleep."

"Almost. There was one last thing I needed to tell you."

"What's that?"

"You need to make an excuse about not going to the Church of the Holy Sepulchre tomorrow morning."

"Huh? Why is that?"

"We need to be in Beit Lahia."

Esty sat up. "Seriously?!"

Forty

LIYAH WOKE TO a light tapping on Esty's bedroom door. She glanced over at Esty who was still asleep.

"Yes?"

"Is that you Liyah? Esty's dad asked in a hushed tone. "You girls going to sleep all day? Your dad and I will be leaving soon to go into town, and Hanna has been up a while."

"Uh, why don't you all go in? Es is still sleeping. We'll join you as soon as we can. It's only a short walk."

"Suit yourself. No worries."

Liyah listened as he descended the stairs. A few minutes later she heard the click of the front door latch. She sat up, reached over, and shook Esty's side until she woke up.

"Wha–?" Esty grunted.

"Time to go. We'll need to get back as fast as possible, so they won't miss us."

Esty sat up, groggy. "Huh?"

"We're going to Beit Lahia, remember?"

"Oh. I thought that was a bad dream I had."

"No, but it will be if we don't get moving. I'll use the bathroom first while you wake up."

Esty heard the door open, then shut again. She rested her head back on the pillow.

Liyah returned fifteen minutes later. "Es," she said loudly. "C'mon. Get a move on. I'll go down and make some breakfast. Let's go. And wear the leather jacket and keffiyeh…for your own safety."

She pulled the shade fully up to let the morning sun stream into the room, then made her way downstairs.

Esty entered the kitchen as Liyah was setting a pitcher of orange juice on the table, between two bowls of oatmeal. She sat down and waited for Liyah to join her.

"You know how to get around in here. Thanks for making breakfast."

"I feel like I'm your sister or something."

Esty grinned. "Because you are. Now tell me again what's going on, and why we would return to a place we just escaped from."

"Ooray told me that we needed to go back to reassure my mother and Khalib that everything is okay. Apparently, there's been a lot of destruction and most lines of communication have been shut off."

"Ooray? When did you have that conversation?"

"Well, it wasn't a conversation, so much. More like a dream. So, I'm not sure it's really true at all. But we can't take a chance, can we?"

"Oh, here we go. You don't even know if we really need to be there."

"I'm pretty confident."

Esty rolled her eyes. "Oh, well that makes all the difference."

"I'm serious. Something about the hospital being hit…the one Ahmad is in."

"What?"

Liyah stared at Esty, her eyes fixed and her expression deadpan.

The blood drained from Esty's face. "God...I hope it's not true. But how were you planning to get there? No one is going to let us into Gaza, and I can't take the car anyway on some whim. My father would kill me."

"By this." She pulled the glittering Timeless Teardrop pendant from underneath her shirt.

"I thought you said you hadn't done that before?"

"Not without the help of Ooray but remember you and I talked about it. All we have to do is grasp our pendants, hold hands, and one of us thinks about where we want to go. The rest is up to the universe."

"Wonderful," Esty said, frowning.

"No, really. We can do it. What have we got to lose, Es?"

"Our lives?"

"C'mon…"

"All right. But I'm doing this for Ahmad. So, I'll blame you when I'm dead."

Liyah chuckled. "Yeah. I know."

"I need to change, though, so that I'm Nura again…just in case. I'll be right back."

Five minutes later she returned. Each took hold of their necklaces.

"Maybe you should be the one who thinks of the hospital, Es. You spent more time there."

"Okay. She closed her eyes. "I'm thinking of the front entrance at the Al-Amal, at the top of the wide stone steps."

Liyah closed her eyes and squeezed hard on her friend's hand. She began to feel vibrations inside her body and heard a low humming sound, growing quickly louder. She opened her eyes briefly and glanced at Esty. Her image was fading, disappearing into the background. Then suddenly she felt herself fading, as if the very molecules of her body were dissolving. She squeezed her eyelids shut. Then with a *Pop!...* they were gone.

Forty-One

LIYAH FELT A tug on her arm. She blinked her eyes open. Esty, wearing Nura's black and white keffiyeh and trench coat, smiled at her.

"I'll be damned, Liyah! It worked."

Liyah grinned in relief. "I hate to think where we'd be if it didn't. Maybe parts of us would be scattered across Gaza."

The two stood at the top of the steps, to the side. People were buzzing in and out of the big glass doors, men in uniform shouting orders. Across the street the square was in shambles, entire buildings lay in ruin, just piles of rubble. Sirens blared, as ambulances arrived from all directions, carrying the wounded from Gaza City and the towns north.

"Come," said Esty. "Let's find Ahmad."

They passed through the glass doors and fought the throng of panicking people to the front desk. Only a small section of the reception area remained in one piece, the rest lying broken under huge chunks of reinforced concrete. A single receptionist greeted them.

"What's happened," asked Liyah.

"Really? Where have you been? We got hit by a missile yesterday. Half of the building is gone. We lost over a hundred patients and medical staff…and ten babies…some blown to pieces, some burned to death."

"Oh, Allah!" replied Liyah. "We're looking for someone…a boy named Ahmad Aziz."

"Sorry. I can't help you. We are trying to salvage most of the first floor and get equipment and staff up to speed so we can transfer as many patients as possible into that area. Some of the halls on the second floor are being cleared so we can handle patients in them as well. But the upper floors are a disaster. They took most of the hit." She looked at Esty. "There's not much you can do here this time, Nura. I'm sorry."

Esty looked stricken. She yanked on Liyah's hand, dragging her toward the main corridor on the first floor. "Follow me. We need to find Ahmad."

They hustled down each hallway, bumping into staff in white coats who scrambled to get beds set up and equipment hooked to generators. They stepped into each room on either side, hoping to find Ahmad.

Nothing.

They flew up the stairs to the second floor, moving down the main corridor.

Still no Ahmad.

Halfway up the rear hallway Esty spotted someone in jeans bending over a table that separated two empty beds, positioned end to end along the wall.

"Ahmad?" she yelled out, running toward him, "Ahmad!"

He stood up and turned around, just as she thrust herself upon him. He freed himself for an instant, peeling her back, making sure it was who he thought it might be. Then he wrapped his arms around her and kissed her.

"Okay, that's enough," said Liyah, playfully. "I'm here, too, you know."

Ahmad hugged her. "I'm so glad to see you two. Your mom and I have been really worried."

"Well, so have we," Esty replied. "For the last half hour, I thought you were dead."

He smiled. "Nope. Not done yet."

Liyah glanced at the bandage wrapped around his head. "How are you even standing here? Last we knew you were just coming out of a coma."

"I know. I got lucky and recovered quickly. Bad knock on the head but only a slight concussion in the end. I have to take it a little easy, though."

"Yeah, right," Esty replied. "We know that won't happen."

He smiled and they hugged again. "Liyah, your mom told me you were probably trapped in a tunnel. You two will have to fill me in later on the details of how you made it out."

"You've seen my mom?"

"Yeah, I guess you don't know she's been volunteering. She let your dad go to Jerusalem when things started to get really bad here. She's a trooper. She's probably outside assisting the medics find beds for the injured arriving in the ambulances. The IDF soldiers are moving quickly south and taking over the Strip and the casualties are high. You must have seen some soldiers outside and in the lobby."

"I did. But I didn't even think they might be Israeli."

"Yup, and they're hauling anyone away if they think they are connected to Hamas…even some hospital staff and a few of the doctors have even been killed."

"No," replied Esty, incredulous. "Are you kidding? Why?"

"Because of the slaughter Hamas committed in places like Re'im. And because they found the opening to one of the major tunnels right under this building. Seems to be the reason for the missile attack."

Esty and Liyah glanced at each other. "Later," Esty said to Liyah.

"What's that?" asked Ahmad.

"Something for later when we have more time."

"Okay, well I'm just helping out the best I can, hooking up stuff. The Dawn can wait a bit. I'm pretty sure we can get the small press up and running quickly, as soon as we clear the debris and reconstruct some temporary space. But that's not as important as this right now. "

"My dad told Esty and me last night he is doing a special project with her dad to build a new media company out of

Jerusalem. He also mentioned to me that he wants you to be part of it, along with helping rebuild the Dawn."

"Sounds great, Liyah. I think we've got a lot of work to do for our *mission*, as you said Ooray refers to it, and this will all be part of that." He leaned over, plugged in one of the monitors, and turned it on. "I can take a break for a minute, now. Why don't we go look for your mom, Liyah?"

"Sure. I would like that if you don't mind. We'll follow you."

Ahmad led them back to the main lobby, checking the corridors along the way, then down to the lobby.

"She might be in the parking lot by the emergency room entrance. They cleaned up that area a few hours ago and taking some patients in again through there."

He brought them out the main doors then along the walk around the side of the hospital, to the parking lot. "There she is…Mrs. Al-Rahim!" he shouted, waving his arms.

Liyah ran ahead. "Hi, Mama," she shouted, unable to disguise her excitement. She knew her mother was not one usually given to emotion, nor bravery for that matter. But lately, that seemed to be changing, she thought. And she couldn't be more proud.

Esty tugged on Ahmad's arm, pulling him to a halt short of Liyah and her mom.

"What is it?" he asked. "What's up?"

"I can't stay. Liyah and I have to go back, Ahmad."

"What? When?"

"Liyah wants to find Khalib before we do. But right after that."

"Why?"

"We got here that special way, like when Morningstar, Kai Li, and Zack left in the spring…from the Mount of Olives. Remember?"

"Yeah. But why do you have to go back?"

"It's complicated. Liyah said we need to go before our dads miss us, but also because she's not sure how time works when this happens. And she'd rather not experiment yet."

"Okay," He kissed her hard and then smiled. "Bummer. But had to get at least one more in."

She kissed him back. "I know. It's so hard not having enough time together. Sometimes I feel like Juliet, unable to see Romeo because their two families were feuding. Only in our case, it's our countries."

"I know. Not really fair is it?" he replied, wrapping his arms around her waist. "I guess we can only be patient and see each other whenever we get a chance. But we have a lot to do, anyway, don't we? I mean to bring our sides together. You told me once that this place is like a microcosm of the world. If we can fix things here, we can set an example for everyone. I believe that's what we're doing…me with the Dawn and you with your tours of the Old City…and together with Liyah and the others. Isn't that how Ooray said it has to work?"

"Yes, love. You're absolutely right. I'll be thinking of you always and be back as soon as I can." She kissed him.

"I love you, Es."

Forty-Two

LIYAH AND ESTY walked along the side streets toward Liyah's home in Beit Lahia. The morning sun still warmed their faces, even as they moved deeper into the fall season. But dust filled the air, and each block of devastation, dead bodies, wounded stragglers, and mothers searching the rubble for their children weighed on their hearts.

"Your mom says it's like this everywhere," said Esty.

"I feel like I'm losing what country I, and all Palestinians, had left."

"Yeah," agreed Esty. "In a way it makes me feel the same, like we can't fix this. Even our leaders are against us."

"How do you mean?"

"Last spring when I met Ahmad, we used to talk about this all the time. He was doing undercover research for his first article for the Dawn, meeting with Hamas operatives, other radical groups, Yusuf from Saudi—you remember him, my father, and of course yours. He would tell me how countries and factions from inside and outside of Israel and Gaza were trying to disrupt the Levant…it's what led to the confrontation in Jerusalem last spring. With the help of Ooray, we were able to save things from blowing up entirely."

"He was right, Es."

"I know, but he also said that he feared the leaders of Hamas were capable of stirring up more trouble because he believed they never really cared about the Palestinian people or creating a new state for them. They only cared about their own power, and to push the Israelis into the sea. From his standpoint, they were willing to misrepresent Islam, stoke hate, and try to fool the real Palestinian people."

"My father says he was right on that, too. But he hoped Ahmad's fair treatment of the situation in the Dawn would plant the seeds for more understanding between all Israelis and Palestinians. He still believes it can happen…even now."

"But my own country is guilty as well, Liyah. Many of the leaders, like we talked about. They don't care about my people like Hamas doesn't care about yours. They didn't go across the border like Hamas and act in the most vile behavior humans are capable of, but it seems they don't want a two-state solution either, and are intent on pushing Palestinians off the land, like Hamas wants to push us into the sea. Everybody, on both sides, feels their very homeland and livelihoods are at stake. Not because in their heart they hate the other, but because their leaders stir up trouble then use that to stoke the hate.

"Ahmad said that nothing is going to get fixed quickly. There have been broken promises, and multiple cease-fires—not only recently, but for over seventy years. He said there would be more, but that they would stop when the collective goodwill and trust of both sides reached a critical mass. And that will be reached only when the people fire the current leaders."

They turned onto Liyah's street.

"It's why we're on this mission, Es," Liyah replied. "To shine the light on that. To stop it. Let's keep going. Let's fight for it."

They made their way up to the front door and into the house.

"Hello?" asked Khalib, hearing the front door close. He looked up from some papers he had spread out on the table.

Liyah followed his voice into the dining room.

"Hey, little brother."

"Liyah! He stood up and hugged her, then Esty."

"What are you working on, Khalib?" asked Esty.

"A list."

"List?" his sister replied.

"Yeah. Of my friends and other people who we can recruit."

Liyah smiled. "Really."

"Well, I think that little adventure we just went on tipped me over the edge. I felt a bit lazy not doing as much as should be to help you guys over the past six months, and this kinda got me to see even better that no one's gonna fix this crap if we don't show them the way…and gather an army. Ali and Jawad talked my ear off the whole way home. I tried to explain some of what happened, but then even I don't understand everything…you know?" He grinned.

Esty laughed.

"Wasn't expecting you guys so soon," Khalib continued. "Especially you, Esty."

"Ooray's idea," Liyah replied.

"Huh."

"More on that later. Might have been only a dream. I thought I was supposed to get Esty to see Ahmad, and let our mother know I was okay. We just saw her at the hospital. She told us you were at home."

"It's funny you say that."

"Why?"

"Because I had a weird dream last night, too."

"About mom?"

"No. About Ooray. I found myself in Jerusalem, looking up at the top of the Al-Aqsa Mosque. Ooray was up there on top of the mosque again, as an eagle. The eagle turned into flashing colors of light and flew straight at me. I woke up in a sweat."

Liyah chuckled. "Hmm. That *is* weird,"

"Not as weird as what I found on my bureau when I got up. Let me show you." He jogged up the stairs and returned with something in his hand, then handed it to his sister.

Liyah examined it. It was a large silver coin. On one side was an embossed image of an olive tree, the symbol of

Palestine. Above the image was a heart, the symbol of love, and below was the symbol for infinity. She flipped it over. On that side was the embossed image of a fig tree, the symbol of Israel. Above it was a dove with an olive branch, the symbol of peace, and below it, the symbol for infinity, like on the front.

"It's beautiful," said Esty.

"And I believe not without a reason," added Liyah.

"What do you mean?" replied Khalib.

"Ooray…that's what I mean. We can't stay, but can you get this to Ahmad? He knows some printers who also do metal presswork, like for coins. Ask him to get a dozen or so of these made up. They'd be perfect to give to the soldiers in our *army*, as you called it, here in the Levant."

"I get it, Liyah," said Esty, giving her a thumbs up.

Khalib smiled. "Me too." He saluted his sister. "As you wish, my captain."

Liyah cupped the coin in her hands and closed her eyes. A moment later she passed the coin to Khalib and watched his eyes grow wide as energy flowed through his body.

"Well, brother, I wish we could stay. But duty calls. Play with the coin in my absence. I'll teach you when I get back. I think Dad and I will return as soon as he completes a project there, and we feel it's safe enough here. Meantime we'll be with Esty."

She stepped back from the table. "Time to go, Es."

Esty stepped close. They held on to their pendants and reached out to each other. But before Liyah could close her eyes and think of home, she felt a vibration against her wrist. She brought her hand up in front of her. Zack's TrueHeart sapphire charm on her bracelet pulsated its deep blue light. She looked at Esty.

"Shit. Here we go again."

About the Author

Bruce Campelia was born in Boston, Massachusetts, and now resides in St. Paul, Minnesota. He holds degrees in engineering, business, and health, and has traveled extensively throughout America and internationally. He has three daughters and five grandchildren, plays the piano, and is an avid hiker.

Bruce's books weave together mystery, history, philosophy, culture, spirituality, and technology into modern-day adventure-thrillers...with a touch of fantasy.

Find out more at www.lightpassers.com

www.ingramcontent.com/pod-product-compliance
Lightning Source LLC
Chambersburg PA
CBHW060603310726
48982CB00008B/1224/J

* 9 7 9 8 9 8 6 6 6 5 6 4 1 *